LIGHT UP HIS LIFE

THE BRIDES OF PURPLE HEART RANCH BOOK 10

SHANAE JOHNSON

THOSE JOHNSON GIRLS

Edited by Alyssa Breck

Manufactured in the United States of America
First Edition December 2019

"Slow down, Luke. This isn't the Millennium Falcon."

In his peripheral vision, Luke Jackson saw that the green of the trees whizzed by in a blur, much like the end of a *Star Wars* scroll. He lifted his right foot from the gas. Moving it over to the brake pedal, he stomped down. The leaves on the trees became visible as though they'd just shot out of hyperspace.

"Oof."

"You okay?" Luke reached his arm out to brace his friend Paul Hanson. Paul rubbed at the back of his forehead. His head had slammed forward but missed the dashboard. When it slammed back, the back of his head collided with the cushions of the headrest.

"Man, I'm sorry," said Luke, as he pulled over to the side of this road. "I didn't mean to."

Luckily, there weren't many vehicles on the road early this morning. He doubted there were many vehicles on the road at any one time. They were traveling the backroads of Montana. There was nothing but fields and mountains as far as the eyes could see. The countryside was a welcome change from the harsh desert they'd come from.

Afghanistan looked very much like Tatooine, the fictional planet of his namesake Luke Skywalker. Luke's father had named his only son after his favorite science fiction character. No wonder Luke had gone on to be a pilot in the United States Air Force. But that life was over for him now.

Luke had retired from service. He was now ready to start his civilian life in full. He just had one more mission to complete.

"Calm down, buddy." Paul chuckled. "I get that you're used to speed and no one being on your rear in the clouds. But down here on the roads, there is an actual speed limit."

Luke looked up at the white sign on the road. There were only two numbers in black on the sign where Luke was used to doing at least triple digits in the air. He'd performed many a death-defying stunt in his time in the air force. He'd saved many lives in his mission. When he was in the air. The one time his mission put him on the ground, his best friend got seriously wounded.

"You think you might have a concussion?" asked Luke. He put the back of his hand to Paul's head.

"What?" said Paul. "No. I'm fine." Paul slapped at his friend's hand like an annoyed adolescent swatting away a parent who was babying them. He brought his hand from his neck and down lower to rub at his back.

"Is your back bothering you?"

"Luke—"

"Do you need to get out and stretch your legs? We've been driving for more than thirty minutes." Luke reached for the door handle, but Paul reached over and stayed his hand.

"Luke, I'm good."

Those were the same words Paul had said after the explosion rang through their ears. Paul hadn't been good then. He wasn't good now. Luke had walked away from the explosion with only a scratch on his knee from where he'd impacted the ground.

"Look," sighed Paul, "if you must know, I'm just not in a hurry to get to this place."

"Everyone has said it's the best place for an injury like yours."

Paul shook his head, but he didn't argue. That was the problem. Paul had an opinion on everything. But these days, he wasn't arguing much. He hadn't so much given up as he had given in to his injury.

"Three months, that's all I'm asking," said Luke.

"Why three months?"

Luke shrugged. That's what the pamphlet for the Purple Heart Ranch read. *Give us three months to change your life.* Luke didn't need anything in his life changed. He was the luckiest man he knew. He'd survived three tours and only walked away with a scratch. But he'd lost many of his friends. He'd nearly lost his best friend. But he'd managed to save Paul's life.

Paul had limped away with all his limbs attached. But he was in chronic pain every day. Pain changed a man. It took a lot for Paul to laugh and find joy these days. It took a lot for him to want to try to live his life to the fullest.

Paul had been honorably discharged for his injuries. Luke had had a year left in the service at that time. He'd gone to see Paul every time he could. Each time, his friend was more and more a shell of his former self.

"You don't have to stay and babysit me," said Paul.

"Yeah, I think I do. With all the trouble you'll get yourself in if I'm not around."

There was a flicker of amusement in Paul's light gaze. But only a flicker.

Guilt washed over Luke. If he hadn't been there to dive on Paul, his friend might not have made it out unscathed. Might. There was a chance that he could've walked away whole. But because Luke had hefted his bulk and thrown his friend to the ground, Paul had landed on a pipe that caused damage that wouldn't let up on the pain.

"We're here," Luke announced, pulling up to a gate.

"Are you sure?" asked Paul.

There was a curly flower on the gate. The name read The Bellflower Ranch. The purple flower looked much like a heart.

"This is the right address," said Luke.

They'd drove through the gates and realized that they were indeed in the right place. A JROTC regiment practiced drills in the field. Men and women walked with rifles slung over shoulders toward a shooting range. A few men were on horseback. Their buzz cuts and rigid shoulders couldn't hide the fact that they were all military. Neither could the prosthetic limbs many sported.

This was the Purple Heart Ranch. A place for wounded soldiers to convalesce and get their lives back. Hopefully, they could help Paul get back to a good place.

Luke parked the car. He stopped himself from hurrying around to the other side to let Paul out. He knew it wouldn't be appreciated. It also was an unmanly thing to do, and Paul would ridicule him ... for longer the second time.

"You must be Major Solo."

A blond-haired soldier marched up to him. His gait was off. Luke looked down to see why. His right leg was a prosthetic. Beside him was an older man with golden-honey skin and a serene smile like a Buddha statue.

"Oh, I get it. Luke and Han. *Star Wars.*" The young blond soldier turned to the older man who clearly didn't get it.

That was a running joke in the service. And the monikers were true to characters. Luke had been the golden boy who could pull off impossible missions. Han had the swagger and got all the girls. Or at least he used to. But his swagger was off with his chronic back and hip pains.

"I'm Sergeant Dylan Banks."

"You're the one in charge?" asked Luke after shaking the man's hand.

Banks shrugged. "As much as anyone could be in charge of a herd of wildcats."

"This is Dr. Patel, the ranch therapist. He works with your internal wounds."

The old man had a friendly grin and kind eyes. But they were focused on Luke instead of Paul, the actual patient.

"Welcome," said the doctor. "We're glad the two of you will be staying with us."

"Oh, I'm not staying," said Luke. "I've found a place off the ranch in town."

"Nonsense," said Banks. "Each unit has two bedrooms. The second room is unoccupied. You're welcome to it."

That hadn't been part of the plan. Luke had work of his own to do while his friend healed. But if he stayed, he could low-key spy on Paul's progress. Paul shook his head like he saw Luke's plan clearly.

"You're welcome to take part in the activities as well," said Dr. Patel, his serene gaze still fixated on Luke instead of Paul.

"Absolutely," said Banks. He addressed the one of them with the actual problem. "We have physical activities, such as horseback riding, which I think will help with your hip and back. It certainly helped with me."

Banks indicated his prosthetic leg. The idea of riding horses did intrigue Luke.

"We also have mental health activities, which Dr. Patel leads."

"Oh, I don't think I'll be needing that," Luke said.

Both men raised their brows at Luke, as though he was an addict holding a bottle of whiskey in his hand while denying his problem.

"I'm not injured," Luke said. "I'm here to support Paul. And to finish my latest book."

"Wait, you're the pilot that writes the Military Science Fiction under the name Walker Skye."

"Yeah, that's me."

It was still strange for him when people praised his books. Mainly because he'd had to keep his literary activities quiet while he was active.

Luke's stories took place in another time and dimension, but war was a universal language. He had to avoid the appearance that he was disparaging his superiors in divulging secrets. Hence, the pen name.

"I love your books," said Banks. "So do a lot of

the kids in the JROTC program. Will you talk to them?"

"I wonder if you would be willing to do a talk at the local library?" asked Patel. "It's difficult for kids to get out here. I think a lot of young people and older men would love to meet you and have a reading."

Luke hadn't done a talk before. He hadn't gone out as his pen name. Now that he was a full-time author, this would be expected of him. What better place to practice than here?

CHAPTER TWO

There was nothing like the smell of old books. Musty, like something aged and left under a protective sheet for years, with a bit of manured earth and a touch of human sweat. Elaine reveled in it.

That combination could only be found in a library. There wasn't the old smell there as most bookstores featured newly printed materials that were on some bestselling lists curated by people who only cared about what was popular at the moment. Those people didn't take into account what had been popular a hundred years ago. Or what had stayed the test of time.

Elaine clicked on the lights of the library. The stacks illuminated one by one. Dust mites swirled as she turned on the air conditioner. She sneezed into her hand at the gathering dander and smiled.

No, there were no new books in this section. These weren't the books that were pristine and purchased by one person to covet. Every volume had been through the trenches. Shared, paged through, returned, only to be picked up by someone new to experience what was between the pages.

Well, some of the books had taken that journey. Many of the cards at the backs of the books of the classics had only a handful of checkouts. Or none.

But they would always have a home in the library. That's what libraries were for. Homes for books, where people showed up to take them out and were fined if they forgot to bring them back. If only it were that way during her parents' divorce. Then their remarriage. And then their second divorce.

Elaine walked to the front door of the town library and flicked open the lock. There was no line waiting outside to come in and snatch up a book. It was nine in the morning.

At noon, she was still the only person in the library. The shelves had been dusted. Book jackets stood straight with no slouching at the ends. Reading list books stood faced out waiting to be picked up. But no readers had arrived yet. Elaine sat behind the circulation desk, arranging and rearranging pens. She tugged at her cardigan, smoothing the warm fabric around her shoulders to find warmth in the chilly atmosphere.

"I have great news."

Elaine nearly fell out of her chair at the voice that came from behind her. Mary was the head librarian here. She'd gotten the job right out of college. Mainly because the last head librarian had been her aunt. Nepotism ran rampant in this small town.

"I just got a call from Pastor Patel," Mary continued, not noticing Elaine's heart attack. "He said Walker Skye is in town, and he's open to coming and doing a reading here."

"Walker Skye?"

The name did not ring a bell.

"You know who he is. He writes military science fiction. He hit the bestseller's list earlier this year."

Elaine still didn't know who this person was, but she knew of that genre. She wasn't a total literary snob. She enjoyed speculative fiction. But space wars? Really? What kind of value did that add to literature? None.

"I don't think he's ever done a reading or a

signing," said Mary. "This is going to be so popular with the younger group. For the last year, we can't keep his books on the shelf."

Mary walked over to the bestselling books section, a section Elaine always neglected. She could see one of the offending books from here. Very few of those books had been turned faced out this morning. Mary frowned, turning one particular cover outward-facing.

A big old space ship was on the front cover. Vibrant colors splashed the jacket. The bold colors hurt Elaine's eyes.

"Looks like someone neglected her shelving duties this morning," said Mary.

Someone hadn't. Someone had spent time on the books that mattered, the books that shaped human thought, the books that changed lives. Though most people in this town preferred things the way they always were.

Elaine pinched her lips. "If we don't showcase the classics like we do the bestsellers, how can we expect people to pick them up?"

"Elaine, honey, you have to remember; the classics make kids think of school and homework. The bestsellers like Walker Skye make them think of downtime, relaxation, and entertainment. Which would you grab for after a long day of work?"

Elaine opened her mouth, but Mary stopped her.

"Don't tell me. I already know what you're going to say. Something by Hardy or Eliot or Austen."

Contrary to popular convention, Elaine was not an Austen fan. Sure, *Pride and Prejudice* and *Emma* were classics. But the stories were wholly unrealistic. The one where the wealthy guy fell for the plain, poor girl. Or the other one where the wealthy guy falls for the penniless girl. Like any of them would stay together. But Elaine held that unpopular opinion to herself.

"Not everyone is like you, Elaine. Not everyone finds joy in five hundred page literary tomes that aren't *Harry Potter*."

Elaine rolled her eyes again. She never got the *Harry Potter* draw. It was just *The Lord of the Rings*. But written for children.

They were walking by the romance section. Mary's favorite section. Elaine avoided this section like the plague. The short books were even more unrealistic than Austen or Rowling. Love that happened in just a couple hundred pages was doomed to fail after the last page. A book could end with a happily ever after. But no books ever showed what happened after the happily ever after began. After the last page was where the hard work started, and that's where the fairytale fell apart.

"Look, I know I'm not going to convince you of this," said Mary. "But we need this kind of attention. Attendance is down here. If we can't increase circulation, then the county will target staff for upcoming budget cuts."

Elaine still had objections. But she couldn't argue that one. Either get the *Star Wars* author in here or risk losing her job. She would simply have to practice holding her tongue while the old guy espoused the virtues of space warfare.

"Why don't you take your lunch break," said Mary. "It's taco Tuesday, your favorite."

Elaine was nothing if she wasn't a creature of habit. She liked her routines, just like she liked knowing the end of the stories she was reading.

"No, it's *your* favorite," Elaine countered.

"That's right." Mary grinned, reaching in her pure for cash. "Could you bring me back a chicken taco with extra guac?"

"Sure, Mary."

CHAPTER THREE

So this was small-town America. The convenience stores were named for a family instead of the normal chain stores that broadcast commercials during morning television. The diners and restaurants also had family names; O'Malley's Pub, Castro's Mexican Cuisine, Patel's Family Restaurant.

Walking down the main street of the town, Luke was greeted with delectable smells, friendly smiles, and welcoming mats at every turn. After years in hostile territory, he could get used to this.

He wandered into the town's only bookstore. It too wasn't a chain, not that there were many bookstore chains left now that much of human literature and entertainment could be held in the palm of the hand. Still, the internet age was alive and well in this quaint town.

Satellites outnumbered the phone lines up above. A couple of phone carrier outlets were tucked into the two gas stations and smaller corner stores he'd passed by on his walk. Cell phones were in the hands of the young and the old. Unfortunately, he didn't see anyone walking the sidewalks carrying a paperback.

There was a book in the hands of the woman across the street at a diner. She held a hardback book to her nose. He could tell by the title on the cover that it was classic British Literature straight out of Advanced English class.

Luke had never liked those books in school. They never ended happily. Usually, it was the heroine who suffered some moral punishment that was all the hero's fault.

The woman with her nose in the book was quite pretty. Brown hair pulled back in a bun. A pert nose. Glasses covering her brown eyes. She looked like a stereotypical librarian. Not a real one, more like a young woman who was trying to dress the part, complete with a pastel cardigan. Only she was more pretty than bookish.

There had been a ton of librarians back in Luke's

hometown. His upscale neighborhood in Northern Virginia had had a library within every five miles. All the librarians there looked the same. Like doting grandmothers or spinster aunts pushing books into the hands of impressionable youths.

The grandma-librarian types were thrilled that kids were reading and didn't try to censor the titles. They'd push dragon books, science fiction books, war books, anything that the kid was guaranteed to open.

The spinster-aunt looking ones were a different case. They often hid the bestselling titles. They shamed teenage girls from reaching for the romance novels. They tsked at the young men who reached for covers with spaceships and guns.

Luke's days were planned around the librarian's shifts. He knew when the grandmas were there behind the circulation desk and when the aunts patrolled the stacks.

The woman in the dining window turned the page. She reached for a napkin and placed it between the pages before setting the book down and taking a bite of her taco. The innards of the taco spilled down on the plate and her dress, which she'd covered with a napkin.

So, not only was she pretty, she was careful with

the book. She'd taken great pains to separate the taco. And she wasn't a dog-earring reader. She wouldn't appreciate Luke. Dog ears helped him not only remember his place, but it also helped him remember the best parts of the book. When he saw that crease, he could go back and reread the best parts.

Though the bibliophile fascinated him, Luke turned away from the diner and the window. A relationship was not in his cards. He had work to do and a friend to look after.

He knew survivor's guilt was a form of PTSD. And he was doing something about it. He was getting his friend the help he needed. Once Paul was situated, then Luke would start to date again. Maybe he'd set his sights on the library. He'd be sure to bypass the town's spinster aunties and ask the kind-looking grannies for their granddaughters' phone numbers. Surely they would have taught their young ones the beauty of the written word.

The town's library was quite small compared to all the libraries in his home town. It was the size of a small house where the libraries back in Northern Virginia had been as big as department stores, often with two floors. Walls and walls of books, CDs, movies, video games, magazines, even toys that kids could check out.

This library was one room. Wall to wall shelves covered each corner. And there were five stacks in the middle of the room. A row of tables sat off to the side. Two young people sat at one with iPads out.

Well, the young woman had her iPad out and was tapping away. The young man had a book with the rear of a spaceship and its thrusters glowing brightly on the cover.

"Would you put that down?" said the young woman. "We have serious literature to do a project on. I don't want you talking about photon guns when we're supposed to talk about morality and feminism in the Victorian era."

The young man peaked over the cover of the book. "This book is actually filled with feminism. Did you know the captain of the ship is a woman? And the sexes are equal in this future. In the military, men and women even share the same bunks and bathrooms."

Luke took a closer look and saw that the young man was reading his first book. Although the military wasn't that advanced, Luke had served with many women in the service who were his betters.

The creation of his heroine was dedicated to the female pilot who'd taught him everything he knew.

The book had been a hit, and he'd gotten a four-book deal. It was the third book that he was supposed to be writing now. But it had stalled during Paul's recovery.

"Can I help you find something?"

Luke turned to the circulation desk. There wasn't a gray-haired, rosy-cheeked granny sitting there. Neither was this woman quite the spinster auntie type.

She would definitely be classified as young and beautiful. She didn't dog-ear the pages of the book she'd been reading. She didn't stuff a napkin or bookmark to hold her place either. This librarian laid her book down with the covers open and the pages pressed into the desk. The book was clearly a women's fiction book.

"Yes," said Luke. "Dr. Patel sent me. About doing a reading."

Her eyes remained blank. And then they lit up. "You're Walker Skye?"

Luke nodded.

Behind him, the young man reading his book turned and gaped.

Luke hated this part. He didn't like to be the

center of attention. He preferred to have his characters do that. Why had he agreed to this?

"I'm Mary, the head librarian here. We are so thrilled to have you."

Luke mustered a smile. He'd never been a charmer when it came to ladies. Probably because he never looked at them as objects of desire. Having been around military families his whole life, women were either caretakers in the home or defenders on the battlefield, often both. Asking women to cover his back was no problem. Asking one on a date had always been a challenge for him.

Mary, the librarian, was looking at him with interest. But he didn't feel the same pull toward her. Not like the taco-eating, classic book reading woman back at the restaurant. Luke wasn't sure what drew him to her? By their reading tastes and place holding habits, they had nothing in common. Though he did like Mexican food.

"Mr. Skye?"

Luke blinked to find the young man with his book, and a pen extended to him.

"I'm so sorry for bothering you."

"It's no bother at all," said Luke.

He beamed. "Could I get your autograph?"

"That's a library book, Daniel," said Mary, the librarian.

Daniel's face fell.

"Tell you what," said Luke. "I'm giving a reading here in a couple of days. You come to the reading, and I'll bring you an autographed copy."

Daniel's face lit up.

Luke made the arrangement for his reading. Mary made advances that he dodged like he was in a fighter jet. They exchanged numbers, but he only had the intention of using hers for business purposes if the need arose. He doubted it would.

With a wave to the young man who still wasn't typing on his iPad along with his classmate, Luke exited the library. He needed to get some writing done. He suddenly had a hankering for tacos. He hurried down the street, back toward the Mexican restaurant. But he stopped in the bookstore first. He figured he'd support the local economy and buy his book there to autograph instead of going into his personal stash. He was already feeling like a part of the community.

CHAPTER FOUR

Elaine brushed the salsa from her blouse. This was why she always wore dark colors. Food, drinks, pen markings inevitably ended up on her clothing. It was also why she always kept a cardigan handy to wrap around her shoulders and cover the evidence.

She wasn't clumsy. She just was careless with anything that wasn't parchment. Fabrics shuddered when she pulled them onto her body. Each article of clothing knew their time in her closet would be short-lived.

But the books on her shelves got the utmost care. Weekly dusting. A heavy curtain over the window to protect them from light. Thick comforters on her bed, so that the books didn't suffer the dreaded AC unit being on for too long or at all.

A side of chips and guacamole appeared before her on Elaine's table. She looked up to see Juan Castro grinning down at her.

"On the house," said Juan.

Elaine pushed the salty treat back toward him. "No *gracias*."

"Oh, come on, Elaine. It's not an engagement ring."

Elaine shuddered and slipped her cardigan over her shoulders. It might as well be. That's how most animal mating rituals began. The male would offer the female the choicest morsels of food. And then he would pounce.

Elaine had no interest in being pounced on. Her belly was full of tacos, which she'd paid for herself. No matter that a good portion of it was on her shirt.

"I'm not even asking for a dinner date, just lunch," said Juan.

"Juan, you know I don't date."

"No woman doesn't date."

"This woman does." Elaine paused, examining her sentence structure. "Doesn't. Whatever. We've been through this before."

Elaine gathered her book. She removed the

napkin from her book and pressed a cloth bookmark between the pages to hold her space. Not that she needed the reminder. She'd read *Tess of the d'Urbervilles* from cover to cover more times than she could count. And the book looked as pristine as the day she'd bought it.

Placing the book carefully in her bag, Elaine scooted out of the booth and around Juan. The man was unrelenting. But she came here every Tuesday for the last four years because the tacos were to die for. She grabbed the to-go bag for Mary, making a mental note that next time it would be Mary's turn to come out for Taco Tuesday to-go.

Mary easily dealt with male attention. Because Mary wanted male attention. Elaine did not.

"I don't think you've dated anyone since high school," said Juan.

He was wrong. Elaine hadn't dated anyone in high school. She hadn't dated anyone in college either. What was the point? More than fifty percent of all marriages ended in divorce. And those that didn't held the two participants trapped in a cycle of unhappiness.

Why bother? All Elaine needed was her books to keep her warm at night. She was happy getting lost in a story where she knew how it ended. And most stories she read ended in tragedy, thus confirming that true love was a made-up concept by the Hallmark Channel.

"Just a coffee," Juan said.

"See you next Taco Tuesday, Juan." Elaine left a tip on the counter and headed out the exit.

The fall air was brisk. She cradled her book to her chest. Her cell phone buzzed in her pocket. Elaine backed up off the sidewalk and under an awning to answer it. She wasn't one to walk and talk, or worse, walk and text. Safety first, especially since she was often carrying one of her precious books in her bag.

Elaine pulled her phone out of her bag to see that it was a text from Mary. "Hurry back," it read. "Exciting news."

Elaine could use some exciting news. Jobs as a librarian were hard to come by in today's world. Many circulation desks were turning digital. Like the science fiction novels she detested, artificial intelligence was taking over her world. If they didn't figure out something to increase circulation at the library and get more bodies into the building, Elaine's job might be in jeopardy in the near future.

"On my way," she texted back. Then put her phone back into her bag.

Elaine waved to a few people she knew as she headed back down the main street. She'd lived in this town her whole life, deciding to stay after her parents' latest divorce. Elaine had gotten the house in the second divorce. It had always been the one constant in her life, and so she'd decided to stick close to it. Her parents were long gone; this town had always felt like home to Elaine. So, she'd staked her roots.

She liked the predictability of small-town living. She liked knowing all of her neighbors. She liked that change moved at a slow progress. Slow she could handle. Fast and unpredictable, she didn't like.

A man was moving slowly across the street. Elaine noted that he was tall, well-built. He walked with his shoulders straight like he had a purpose. His stride was long, sure. But his head was down, so she couldn't see his eyes.

He wasn't looking down at his phone. He was looking down at a book. More than wanting to see what color his eyes were, she wanted to know what he was reading.

A car rounded the corner. The reader was almost out of the crosswalk and to her side of the street. But he wasn't looking up, so he didn't see the car.

It took Elaine a second to make her decision. She

dropped her bag to the ground. Then she dashed out into the street.

Her hands wrapped around his wrists, making sure to cradle the book he held. And then she gave the big man a tug.

They tumbled to the ground. Elaine felt the impact on her shoulders and bottom. She was going to be bruised in the morning. But what hurt most was her head. Her good deed for the day would leave her with a headache for the rest of the afternoon.

Brown. His eyes were brown. That was the last thing she remembered.

That and the title of his book. It was a science fiction book. One where the AI's take over the planet. Fitting.

And then everything went black.

CHAPTER FIVE

Luke paced the linoleum floors of the emergency room. The soles of his shoes peeled off the floor with something sticky each time, trying to hold him in place. He hadn't held still since they'd wheeled her in here.

Elaine was her name. He'd learned that when he'd grabbed her purse from the ground. He'd left behind the taco take-out bag as it was a casualty, and the ants were already on it. Her state ID had slipped from her purse, and he'd seen her name.

He wasn't the only one who knew her name. One of the EMT drivers had known her name, as well. It was a small town. Of course, everyone knew everyone else. He'd given Luke the side-eye. It was the first unwelcome gesture he'd been presented in this town.

He couldn't blame them. It was his fault. He was surprised more people weren't glaring at him from the sidewalk.

The accident had happened after the end of the lunch rush, so not many people had been out. He'd been able to whisk her to a bench and out of the road. The car that had been driving by had out of state plates, which was likely why they hadn't stopped. No ties to this community.

It hadn't been the driver's fault. It had been Luke's fault. He hadn't been paying attention, and she'd tried to save him. Then everything had gone in slow motion.

He'd felt the tug on his wrists. He'd turned, and there she was. She was backlit by the sun. Her hair wasn't all brown. There were golden highlights amongst the strands, and they sparked in the sun's spotlight.

The same golden flecks were in her brown eyes. Like twinkling stars in a hazel galaxy. Luke felt himself being pulled into warp speed. Everything around him went fuzzy, except her clear, sparkling eyes.

Her clear, sparkling eyes that were filled with

alarm. Why was she alarmed? Was she feeling the pull too? She certainly was pulling him toward her.

Only her gaze wasn't filled with passion. It was filled with worry. No, that was fear. Actually, it looked more like terror.

Luke spotted the danger in his peripheral vision. A car was headed straight toward them. She was trying to save him.

Instincts took over. He swung their bodies around so that he was closest to the danger. But in doing so, she landed on her side. His body wasn't able to cushion her blow. The sparkles in her eyes dimmed, then went out as she closed them and lay unconscious.

He just wished it had been him unconscious on the street and not her.

She was still unconscious when the ambulance arrived. She was unconscious the whole ride. Though they'd let Luke ride with them.

"Mr. Jackson, your girlfriend has been moved to a room."

There was also that. In order to ride with Elaine in the ambulance, he'd had to tell a bit of a lie. Luke didn't hesitate to mislead the paramedic. He had no intention of letting Elaine out of his sight now that he was paying attention.

"Is she all right?" he asked as he followed the nurse.

"It just looks like a concussion. Nothing is broken. She should wake up soon."

Luke exhaled. But not fully. He wouldn't let go of his full breath until she walked out of the hospital on her own two feet. He didn't plan to leave until then.

The nurse led him into a room. There were two beds separated by a thin curtain. On one side of the curtain lay an older woman, snoring lightly. And then Luke saw her, Elaine.

She looked peaceful with her eyes closed. Like an angel dressed in blue and white polka dots. She made the hospital gown look like the height of fashion.

On the table sat her belongings. There was the bag with her book poking out. Luke tore his gaze away from her face and picked up the book.

Thomas Hardy's *Tess of the d'Urbervilles* was not one of Luke's favorites. He didn't like books where the decks were stacked against the protagonists. True, he wrote books about the underdog. But in his books, the protagonists eventually won and defeated the evil empire. Hardy didn't always play by those rules.

But it would seem those rules followed Luke around. This wasn't the first time someone else had suffered because of him. First, his mother. Then Paul. And now her.

A soft moan escaped Elaine. Luke went to her immediately. He held his breath while her eyes fluttered and then opened.

She stared at him. He stared at her. He held still as her gaze flicked over him, and he waited for recognition. And finally, there was a sparkle in her eye.

Luke's heart skipped a beat gazing into those coffee-colored supernovas. It was like a shot of adrenaline right into his chest. Her lips parted, and he forgot how to breathe. Her hand lifted off the bed, and he felt like he should take a knee, like a knight pledging fealty. Shakespeare rang in his ears, *what satisfaction canst though have tonight?*

"My book," she said.

Luke blinked. She wanted a book. No, he wanted her book. Her *Tess* book. Luke presented it to her like it was the flag from an opponent he'd just bested in a joust.

Elaine examined the book, brushing her fingers over the cover. She sighed as she cradled the book to her chest. Luke felt intensely happy as if he'd just given her the world.

"You saved my book," she said.

"You saved my life. We're even. But I'm afraid your taco didn't survive."

"Oh, Mary—ouch."

Elaine had tried to rise from the bed. But winced the moment her head came off the pillow.

Luke flew into action. At least he would have if he knew what to do. "Should I call the nurse? Do you need medication? Another pillow?"

Elaine rubbed tenderly at the back of her head. "No, no. There's just a bump here."

"I'll get the doctor," he said. "They should run more tests."

"For a bump on the head? I'm sure I'm fine."

Luke wasn't so sure. Before he could reach for the door, an older gentleman came in.

"Hello, Elaine. Pretending to be a superhero, I hear?"

"Just doing my civic duty, Dr. Brady," she said.

"It was my fault," said Luke. "I was looking down at—"

"Your cell phone?"

"No," both Luke and Elaine said at the same time.

"He was looking down at a book," said Elaine.

"Sounds like something you would do," the doctor said to Elaine. "I've brought your discharge papers. And one of the nurses let Mary know you're here and that you're fine. She said to take the rest of the day off, obviously. You're free to go when you feel up to it."

"Free to go?" said Luke. "Have you done a cat scan? X-rays?"

"There's no medical need for any of those things," said Dr. Brady. "It was just a bump on the head."

Paul's injury started as just a bruise on his back, and now he had chronic pains. Paul just had a twinge in his back before they discovered it was more. Luke's mother had had a few cramps and dizzy spells before she'd been taken by her ailment. There could always be something more lurking beneath the surface.

"Just take a few aspirins, and you'll be right as rain in the morning," said the doctor.

'Thank you, Dr. Brady."

"Shouldn't she at least be under observation?" asked Luke.

"You look after her tonight then," said the doctor. "You're qualified as her boyfriend."

And with that, he ducked out into the hall. The older woman on the other side of the curtain continued snoring lightly. Luke turned to face Elaine slowly. He sensed he was turning to face a firing squad. He was right.

Her narrowed gaze and pinched expression confirmed his suspicions. "Did he say you're my boyfriend?"

CHAPTER SIX

*E*laine's head throbbed. Her mouth was a bit fuzzy, and the words didn't feel right on her tongue. They also didn't sound completely coherent to her ears.

She'd been dreaming of dancing at a May fair. Tess had met the man she would fall in love with at the fair. In the book, Tess had made eyes with Angel Clare across a bonfire. Elaine was making eyes with a man in her dream. Only instead of across a bonfire, he'd been standing across a street. And there was no one else there dancing. There were just cars between them as they flirt-gazed at one another.

She'd opened her eyes to see the man she'd been flirting with in her dreams standing over her. His gaze wasn't saying come hither. It was filled with compassion and care. She might be delirious, but there looked like a hint of devotion. Which was madness. She didn't know this man. But she did know that any man looking at a woman he did not truly know with devotion would only spell her doom. It said so in her favorite book, which he was holding.

And then it all came back to her. But what she was still having trouble understanding was why anyone would think he was her boyfriend.

She did not date. She had no plans to ever date or marry or lose her heart to the madness of love. But Dr. Brady was already gone, and she was left with him.

"Elaine ..."

And he knew her name. This man who people thought was her boyfriend. Which he clearly was not. She didn't date. She didn't even know his name.

"Let me explain."

He came closer to the bed. She should scoot away. She should call for the doctor. But his gaze held her in place. The only thing between them was the massive tome of *Tess*.

"They would only let me ride in the ambulance if I was in some way related to you. So, I told them I was your boyfriend."

Okay, well, that was logical. She had saved his life and his book from flattening. It made sense that he'd want to accompany her to ensure she was well. He was showing signs of Angel Clare, the hero of *Tess of the d'Urbervilles* who'd decided to become a farmer to preserve his intellectual freedom outside his family of clergymen. The man looming over her looked like he could be a farmer with his strong arms and broad shoulders. And he'd brought her book along with them to the hospital, so he couldn't be that bad.

"I couldn't let you go by yourself, not when your fall was my fault …"

Logical and responsible. Not at all like Alec d'Urberville, the villainous, manipulative wealthy son who becomes obsessed with Tess. Though Tess rebukes Alec at every turn, he manages to ruin her body and soul. No, this man was no Alec. He looked far too capable and authoritative.

"Not until I knew you were okay."

"I'm okay," Elaine said. There had been an ache at the back of her skull. But since she'd begun listening to his dulcet voice, the pain had ebbed away. She couldn't let him know that. It was entirely logical that a stranger's voice could make her feel better. "Dr. Brady said so."

"Be that as it may, I would feel much better if you stayed in the hospital overnight." He pulled up a chair and sat at her right side. His eyes now on level with hers. "I would stay with you."

That should not have sent a shiver of warmth through her body. Mainly because one did not shiver when they were warm. But shiver she did as the toasty feeling reached down to her toes.

"Are you cold?" He reached for the blanket at the edge of the bed.

Elaine had the absurd notion to snuggle down into the uncomfortable mattress and await this man, this stranger, to tug up the threadbare hospital sheet and tuck her in. She couldn't remember the last time she'd been tucked in. Certainly not by her parents, who were more interested in arguing with one another than paying her any attention.

"I'm not sleeping in a hospital." Elaine sat up and immediately regretted the action. She winced as the pain from her head returned. She winced again when she realized she was wearing only a thin hospital gown, and her legs were bare.

The stranger in the seat rose and confirmed he was far more Angel than Alec when he turned his back. So, he was a caretaker, a gentleman, as well as a book-lover.

"What's your name?" Elaine asked as she slipped on her skirt under the bedsheets.

The man hesitated.

"You don't want to tell me your name?"

"No," he said. "I mean, yes." His shoulders bunched, and he let out a breath. "I just... It's Luke, like the Jedi."

"What's a Jedi?"

His head swiveled around, reminding Elaine of an owl. His eyes were even as wide as the winged creature. She was dressed now, so she knew he wasn't peering at her body as she straightened her blouse.

"Luke Skywalker," he said.

"Oh," said Elaine as she stepped into her shoes. "That's a *Star Trek* character, right?"

Luke made a choking sound. The rest of his body uncoiled until he stood facing her once more.

Elaine got the notion that she'd gotten that answer wrong. "Sorry," she shrugged. "I don't watch much television."

His grimace was slow to melt away. Elaine watched transfixed as it turned from incredulity to amazement. Then he gave her a sheepish smile.

"It doesn't matter," he said. "It's not important. What is important is your health."

She picked up the discharge papers and waved them in front of his nose. "I've got a clean bill of health. Says so right here."

And with that, she stood up. And nearly fell back onto the bed. Luke's arms were around her before her body touched the mattress.

There went that shiver again. Like a warm cup of tea while she was curled up in a window seat reading her favorite book. That's what it was like to be in this man's embrace.

"Where do you think you're going?" he asked.

Elaine gazed into Luke's eyes. They were brown, like hers. But there were small twinkles in them, like stars. She'd read the flowery language of eyes twinkling in the more romantic sections of books. But the twinkle always faded away by the third act. Elaine stepped out of his embrace, and he let her go but continued to stand too close to her.

"Home," she said. "It's been a long day. I want to take that aspirin and go back to sleep."

"Back to sleep after a concussion?"

"Look Skywalker—"

"It's Luke."

"Luke. It was just a bump. It could've been much worse. I'm lucky I live in the twenty-first century.

Back in the Victorian age, a scratch could mean certain death."

"A bump could be something different beneath the surface," said Luke.

"But it's not. I'm fine. And I'm glad you're fine. I'd say keep your head out of those dangerous books while you're walking, but then …" Elaine held up her own book. "I'm guilty of that, too."

Elaine stepped around him, but he reached for her. He only rested his fingertips on her forearm. But the light touch was enough to stop her in her tracks.

"I ruined your lunch," he said. "Let me take you to dinner."

"I've got food at home."

"Let me take you home."

"It's within walking distance."

"Let me walk you."

Elaine took a deep breath. If she'd known that when she'd saved this man's life that he'd attach himself to her, then she would have … well, she still would've done it. The best thing for her to do was to set the record straight.

"Luke, you know you're not really my boyfriend, right?"

Something passed over his features. Something that made Elaine take in a tiny inhale of breath and hold it. His gleaming brown gaze flicked over her, going from the top of her head, down to her toes, and back up again until their gazes connected. Once again, Elaine felt that heat. But it wasn't a shiver this time. It felt like tiny bursts of fire sparking all over her skin, like Fourth of July sparklers.

"You should also know that I don't want a boyfriend," she said when she found her voice. "I don't date."

Luke frowned. "You don't date?"

"Nope. I philosophically disagree with it."

His grin wasn't predatory. It was curious. But Elaine felt like she was caught, even though she was the one closest to the door.

"Like ever?" he asked.

"Like never," she confirmed.

"Well, that's perfect," he said. "Because I'm awful at dating."

His smile was genuine. So, why did Elaine feel a sense of disappointment that he wasn't pushing the issue? He looked perfectly happy to not date her.

"I still want to take you out," he said. "As friends. A thank-you-for-saving-my-life dinner. You can't say no. I owe you my life."

"You said we were even."

"I forgot to add on the tip."

CHAPTER SEVEN

"You have a date?"

"It's not a date," Luke said to Paul when he got home later that night.

The walk to Elaine's home was uneventful, mainly because he kept his mouth mostly shut. He wasn't sure if the silence was awkward or companionable. He was far too busy watching for any signs of stress or strain from her. But her gait was steady. She didn't wobble or miss a step.

She wouldn't let him call an Uber. Apparently, there weren't any in this small town. There weren't taxis either. Either you walked, or you called someone for a ride. Most people didn't need a ride unless they were going out of the town to one of the farms or ranches.

So, they'd walked.

Elaine had winced when she'd climbed the steps to her small brownstone. Luke had balled his hands into fists so that he wouldn't reach out to her. He'd been around enough wounded soldiers to know the high price of pride. But he had stayed one step behind her in case he needed to catch her.

Was it wrong that part of him had wanted her to fall back into his arms so that he could hold her again?

"It's not a date," Luke repeated, but to himself this time. "It's a thank-you dinner."

"Because she saved your life?" said Paul.

"Yeah."

"From a book?"

"I was reading a book while walking into the street."

"What book?" Maggie Banks, Dylan's wife, spoke up from the kitchen counter. She was lifting food out of Tupperware and placing it onto plates. Paul's fridge was stocked with foods for days after a few of the wives, and their husbands, had stopped by to introduce themselves. Maggie's offering was hot dogs and chicken nuggets.

"It was my book," said Luke. "I'd grabbed a copy

from the local bookstore to sign for a young man I met at the library."

"Dylan got me to read your first book," said Maggie as she pulled out ketchup and mustard. "I was surprised I liked it. I'm not usually one for space wars, but I loved the underdog story."

Of course, she did. There were dogs running all under her feet.

"I only wished there was a love story," Maggie said.

"There is a love story," said Luke.

"Her true love died before the story starts," Maggie protested. "It's been two books. I think she should fall in love again. Don't you?"

Luke pursed his lips. Every female reader he came across had this same complaint. It wasn't enough that a female heroine led a ragtag army to victory in two books. They weren't satisfied until someone's heart was on the line.

"Well, Luke only writes what he knows," said Paul, "and he's never been in love."

"You've never been in love?" asked Maggie.

"No, I haven't," said Luke, glaring over Maggie's head at Paul. "But I know what it looks like."

That sobered his friend up. Paul knew the love story of Luke's parents, along with its tragic ending.

"Your father was a widow?" said Maggie.

Luke nodded.

"He never found love again after your mother passed?"

"He didn't see a need to. Some kinds of love only happen once, especially that kind that hits you square in the eyes and knocks you off your feet. When that happens, it's typically just the one time."

"Sounds like this woman knocked you off your feet," said Maggie.

She certainly had. Quite literally. Elaine was a small thing, too. It was a wonder she'd managed it.

But Luke knew he wasn't in love. This was simply an attraction. Possibly gratitude.

No, it was definitely an attraction. He'd felt a tug of something when he'd seen Elaine earlier in the day, sitting in the restaurant reading that tragic book. He'd felt it when she'd tugged him out of harm's way, and the sun spotlighted her beauty. He saw it again when she woke in the hospital.

"He knocked me square off my feet," said Paul, "and I'm not in love with him."

Luke shot Paul a dirty look. Paul leaned back in his chair with a cheeky grin.

"What's her name?" asked Maggie.

"Elaine. Elaine Reynolds."

"Ohhh," Maggie grimaced.

"What?" asked Luke. "Why, ohhh?"

"Well, the thing about Elaine—"

Maggie didn't get to finish telling him the thing about Elaine. The dogs began to bark as two other women came into the back door. Luke had learned quickly that knocking on doors was not a habit on the ranch. Neither was locking doors.

Two other wives entered the back door carrying plastic containers. Luke was momentarily diverted by the smell of curried spices as Ruhi Jeffries, another wife here but also the daughter of Dr. Patel, came into the back door. At her back was Ginger Collins, another wife, but also the state senate representative.

The conversation halted for five whole minutes as the women shuffled around the kitchen, making their own pleasant conversation, fussed over Paul, and piled more food into the refrigerator.

"What's the thing about Elaine Reynolds?" Luke prompted Maggie at the first lull in the friendly banter.

"Elaine Reynolds?" asked Ginger. "I remember her from high school. I haven't seen her in forever."

"She's still working at the library," said Ruhi. "I

see her when I take the kids in to study. It's the quietest place in town."

"I remember she always used to have her head in a book," said Ginger

"But only the tragedy books," said Ruhi. "Like the ones we had to read as part of English class, she'd read them for fun. More than once."

Was that it? Was that the thing about Elaine? She was a lover of classic literature?

"Is she still not dating?" asked Ginger.

"I don't think so," said Ruhi. "I know Juan has been after her since she got back from college, and she always turns him down."

"Well, Luke here has a date with her," said Maggie.

"It's not a date," said Luke.

"Which is a good thing because Luke is terrible on dates," said Paul.

"Why is he terrible?" asked Ginger.

Before Luke could defend himself, his best friend, who was taking way too much pleasure out of this, continued. "His palms sweat for one. He always winds up spilling something on himself, or on the date. And he can never close the kiss. He can't read signals."

Luke opened his mouth. But he had nothing. All

of that was true. Paul smirked, knowing he'd spoken nothing but facts that Luke couldn't dispute. Luke always felt like it was his first time in the cockpit when he was around a woman he liked. And the flight always ended with him crashing and burning. Whereas Paul Hanson could swagger onto the scene with confidence, brandishing his blaster pistol, and having the women fall at his boots.

"We can help," said Maggie.

"Maggie, you've never been on a first date in your life," said Ruhi. "The first time you met Dylan, he proposed a marriage of convenience."

"And look where I am now," said Maggie, brandishing the rock on her left hand. "Besides, the same thing happened between you and Sean, and look at the two of you."

"I've had plenty of bad first dates," said Ginger. "I can help."

"It's not … I'm not …" But the women were all talking over Luke, planning out his first date with Elaine. He had to wait for another lull in the banter before he could ask the question that plagued him. "So, why doesn't she date?"

Maggie shrugged. "I remember that her parents went through a really nasty divorce. When she was a kid, Elaine was at the library every day until they closed."

"Then she would come to the church until late," said Ruhi. "She'd be reading in the pews during evening service. That probably had something to do with it."

"But she's really smart," said Ginger.

"And really pretty," said Ruhi.

"She loves books," said Maggie. "And you write books. This is a match made in heaven."

"Wait," said Luke. "Slow down. The woman doesn't want to date, but you all are trying to match us like we're going to get married."

Not a single one of the wives denied the statement. They were all sizing him, as though they were taking his measurements for his wedding tuxedo.

Luke looked around for Paul and realized his friend had already made it out the back door, moving faster than his injured hip should allow. He was stuck in a room full of female matchmakers on a ranch where soldiers were known to tie the knot within three months. He was in trouble.

But, for some reason, he didn't run.

CHAPTER EIGHT

Despite being extremely tired after the day's events, Elaine couldn't sleep that night. She couldn't shake the feeling that she was being watched. Hazel brown eyes peered back at her. The eyes reminded her of the browning of a first edition book. There were stories in those eyes. They whispered to Elaine to open the covers, crack the spine, and get comfortable in her favorite reading chair.

The watchful gaze wasn't threatening. It was welcoming. So, why couldn't she sleep?

Probably because she did want to know the story within Lieutenant Luke Jackson's sparkling brown eyes.

Elaine threw the covers off and got out of bed.

The dull ache in her skull didn't allow her to get too far. What if he was right? What if there was more damage than the doctor's saw? There had to be if she was thinking about Lieutenant Jackson and feeling something close to anticipation for their thank-you dinner in twelve hours.

Twelve hours? How was she going to pass the time? Mary had insisted she take the day off to rest and recover. So, Elaine did what she did at nights and on the weekends, she pulled open an old book.

Lieutenant Jackson had saved her copy of *Tess of the d'Urbervilles*. Elaine was still a little surprised that she'd risked her treasured book to save his life. But only a little.

Elaine opened the book. She was just at the part of the story where Tess met the man she would marry. Elaine settled down to read the slow burn love develop between Tess and Angel Clare while the two worked on a dairy farm. Elaine turned the page, knowing that at the end of this chapter. Angel would propose to Tess. Elaine also knew that Tess would hesitate to accept Angel's offer because of the dark secrets of her past that involved the villain Alec d'Urberville.

There were always dark secrets in people's past. Those secrets were what come back to wreak havoc.

In any love story. Her parents had tons of secrets; secret affairs, secret bank accounts, secret trips, secret secrets.

At this point in Tess's story, Elaine always had to push herself forward. Hardy rarely wrote happily-ever-afters. He spoke about real life. That's why Elaine enjoyed his tales.

They spoke of the harshness of class and society, the futility of relationships and love. It didn't matter that Tess's shame wasn't her fault. Human beings did wretched things in the name of love. That's why Elaine avoided the institution at all costs, starting with dating.

Dating was the gateway drug to love. So, Elaine always just said no.

A knock sounded at her front door just as Angel and Tess were confessing their secrets after their wedding. Angel has told Tess about an affair he had with a woman in his youth. Tess has accepted this and then tells her dark secret; that she was assaulted by Alec and delivered his stillborn baby. Elaine placed her bookmark at the passage where Angel says he can't get past Tess's shame, and their love begins to crumble. Elaine decided to let the lovers linger in the possibility that their love would last for a few minutes and went to open the door.

The sun was low in the sky as she pulled open the door. The day was nearly over. She had gotten so lost in the story.

"How are you feeling?" Mary stood on the stoop.

"Fine," said Elaine. And she did feel fine. That's what a good book with big words and a thought-provoking theme did to the brain.

"They said you saved someone in a car accident?" Mary pushed past Elaine, coming into the house.

"No, I saved a pedestrian from a car accident. He was reading while walking."

"Sounds like a crime you would commit."

Elaine blew a harsh breath. "I would never put my books in danger."

Mary plopped down on the couch. "Who was this pedestrian?"

"A soldier," said Elaine.

"A soldier?" Mary parroted.

"A lieutenant."

"A lieutenant?

Elaine knew what was coming next, and she blamed all those Harlequins Mary inhaled in-between the stacks. Sometimes three a day. Those slim, lightweight novelettes rotted the brain.

"From the Purple Heart Ranch?" asked Mary. "One of the taken ones? Or a new one?"

"I think he's new."

Mary bounced up on her toes and squealed, which hurt Elaine's head. "This is it. Fate has found you. You know what happens on that ranch."

Elaine had heard the tales of love at first sight and marriages of convenience turning into the real deal up on that plot of land. There were even enemies-to-lovers relationships that had happened recently between a soldier and the new state senator. It all sounded like fairytales. Elaine never read any fairytales.

"I'm not going to the ranch," said Elaine.

"But you're going to see him again. You saved his life."

"He's taking me out to a thank-you dinner."

"A date."

"A dinner."

"What are you going to wear?"

"I hadn't thought about it."

Mary went straight for her closet. She tugged Elaine's cardigans off hangers and tossed them to the ground along with any buttoned-up blouses. Finally, Mary pulled out a summer dress that would show of Elaine's shoulders and bust line.

Elaine backed out of the closet, arms up to ward off her friend and boss. But Mary advanced.

"It's not a date," Elaine insisted. "I don't date, remember."

"Elaine, you can't be alone for the rest of your life."

"I'm not alone. I have my books."

Elaine waved her hand at the tomes taking up half of her closet. She had far more books than she did articles of clothing. Clothes changed with the seasons. They went into and out of style. They needed to be altered or replacements purchased as the body changed.

"I know your parents' divorce was ugly…"

Elaine turned from her friend and began straightening the books on her closet shelves. Unlike clothing, books were evergreen. The stories inside never changed. They always remained the same. And right where she'd left them.

"… but not all relationships are like that."

"What? You mean not ripping out each other's hearts only to use jumper cables so you can feel that euphoria of endorphins over and over again?"

Elaine's parents had gotten engaged ten times before finally marrying. They got divorced three times and were now planning a vow renewal for their fourth marriage. Her parents were addicted to that feeling of love, the racing heart, the rush of adrenaline, that feeling of falling. Elaine had always preferred two feet on the ground and a clear head. She saw from a tender age that her parents were alternately painfully cruel and lovingly suffocating toward each other. What they called it was love. She never wanted any part of that freak show.

"And my life is full," she said. "Just look at my TBR pile."

The pile Elaine indicated was massive tomes that rivaled *War and Peace*. She preferred the Shelly sisters to Austen. *Frankenstein* was her kind of happy ending, the monster crying over his creator's dead body. That was a better approximation of true love in Elaine's eyes.

"And I have my work at the library," she continued. "We need to do all we can to get more circulation."

"Speaking of that, I met Walker Skye the other day. He's going to do a reading and a signing at the library. People are already signing up. Don't roll your eyes!"

Too late. Elaine's eyes had rolled all the way back in her head. She just couldn't understand the draw of space wars. Oh, wait. *Star Wars*. That's what

Lieutenant Jackson had meant. The one with Luke Skywalker. She only knew that because the actor who had played the part had voiced a number of middle-grade books that were shelved at the library.

"Promise me you'll be on your best behavior when you meet him," said Mary.

"What do you think I'll do? Spit on him?"

Mary gave her a knowing look.

"I will use my best manners." Elaine held up her right hand like when she and Mary were in Girl Scouts. But she didn't tuck in her thumb and pinky finger as was custom.

"And smile."

Elaine frowned.

"And make polite conversation."

Elaine grimaced.

"And don't put down his books."

"I can't do that. I haven't ever picked them up. And I doubt I ever will."

CHAPTER NINE

*L*uke arrived at her place five minutes before the appointed time. He was chronically five minutes early, a leftover from his time in the service. If you weren't early, you were late. He was usually fifteen minutes early, but he didn't want to look like a creeper. That was one of the rules the brides of the Purple Heart Ranch instilled in him during their coaching session; be eager, but play it cool. Women can tell the difference.

He'd been sure to wear dark clothing in case he did spill something on himself. He'd been sure to avoid liquids on the drive over. A puddle of mud was in the crack of Elaine's walkway. Luke managed to step over it without incident.

All signs were pointing to good.

He took the stairs, one at a time, to avoid the possibility of tripping over his own feet. Once at her door, he knocked three times. His palms were dry, another good sign.

He knew that technically, this wasn't a date. And that was fine. He really shouldn't be trying to date someone when he had no firm plans of where his life would take him next. His new job of full-time author didn't require him to live in any one place. His main concern was getting Paul back in a good place, whether his friend liked it or not. So, no, Luke didn't need to get into a serious relationship right now.

The door opened, and all his best-laid plans vanished from his mind.

Elaine stood in dark jeans and a simple t-shirt. She was dressed far too casually for their outing to be considered a date. Still, she looked like a knockout nonetheless.

Her hair was pulled back in a messy bun, the way women fixed it when they wanted it to appear they weren't trying too hard, but it was evident that they had. Her makeup was slight as though to look like it wasn't there. Though her lashes were long enough to be wingtips, he could see the outline of the eyeliner there. There was a touch of gloss on her rosy lips, even though her tongue struck out to lick at her lower lip.

This was a good sign, right? When a woman looked as though she hadn't tried real hard, it usually meant she'd had. At least that's what the brides had told him.

Luke's eyes caught and held on Elaine's lip. He watched as it moved, stretching wide and then forming an O and finally pressing closed.

Oh, wait. She had been forming words. She had been speaking to him. What had she just said?

"You look amazing," he said. A compliment was always a perfect response.

"Thanks," she said. "I was going for a comfortable night out with my potential new friend."

"So, I have potential?" Luke waggled his brows, which he hoped looked cute and endearing.

Elaine's brows pulled together, and she leaned back a bit. She reached behind and pulled the door closed. Great, he was already off to the wrong foot with her.

Luke went to follow Elaine down the steps. Unfortunately, he misstepped, and his foot stepped into one of the potted plants.

The brown guts spilled and exposed the plant's

roots. Luke bent to save the plant, just as Elaine bent down as well. Their heads collided.

Elaine's hand went to her forehead. Luke's hands went there, as well. Their fingers intertwined. Their gazes locked.

The wince she'd worn fell away. The sparkle returned to her brown gaze in the pale moonlight. Luke brushed his thumb across her forehead in a windshield wiping motion.

"We've gotta stop bumping into each other," she said.

That was the last thing he wanted to do. Though he didn't relish the small hurt he'd given her. Her skin was satin in his hands. There was no bruise forming on her forehead. He should give her her head back, but he liked the feeling of her in the palm of his hand. It felt right.

Elaine blinked, snuffing out the sparkles. She turned her head. When she did, she broke his hold on her. She reached for and repotted the plant. Luke brushed the dirt off his shoe. The dry dirt turned to mud in his sweaty hands.

"This is a nice looking house," said Luke when they were down the steps and on a level playing field. "Do you have roommates?"

"No, it's my house. It's been mine since I was

twelve. After my parents' second divorce, they tried for split custody. But, instead of me going to my dad's apartment every other day and living out of a suitcase and backpack, the judge made it so that they would take turns and come stay at the house so that I could stay put."

"That was very responsible of them."

Her gaze tracked up to his. "It was my idea. I hated living out of a suitcase, especially when there were mostly books in my suitcase instead of clothes. It was pretty heavy."

"Divorce is hard. Are they remarried?"

"Yes, they are. To each other. This is their fourth time getting remarried. This last one was a destination wedding. I stayed home. I'm a little too old to be a flower girl, don't you think."

The words were flippant, but Luke saw the crinkle at the edge of her eyes. He saw the tug at the corner of her forced smile. Her lashes fluttered, like a wounded bird's.

Elaine hugged her arms around herself in the breezeless night. Luke noted that she alternately scratched at her chest or balled her hands into fists as she talked about her parents.

"What about your parents?" she asked.

"My mother died when I was very young."

"I'm sorry."

Luke shrugged, scratching at his own chest. "I was too young to remember her." He balled his hand into a fist. "She died from complications due to pregnancy."

Elaine's face contorted into horror.

Luke shook his head, hoping to clear the horror. He hoped she didn't ask. He didn't like to talk about it. But he knew that if Elaine asked, he would tell her.

He would tell her how the pregnancy was high risk, but his mother decided it was worth it. He was worth it. He'd tell Elaine how his mother had nearly died delivering him. That she only survived his first year before she succumbed to the ravages of her body.

But Elaine didn't ask.

"And your father?"

Luke scratched at his chest with his balled fist. "He never remarried. He said she was the one. You'd think he'd be bitter that he lost her. But he's not. He says every day that he was blessed to find her. Not everyone finds their true love."

Elaine snorted. Then covered her mouth. "I'm sorry. That was insensitive."

Luke quirked an eyebrow. "Right. You don't believe in love."

Elaine waggled her head. "I believe that people can care deeply for one another. But the concept of love ..." She shook her head instead of completing the sentence. "No, not love. Passion. Passion like that is dangerous. It's a chemical reaction, a rush of endorphins that increases your blood flow and makes your heart race and your breath catch. That's medically dangerous. Who wants to live in that state all their lives?"

Elaine lifted a brow at him. Luke felt a rush of endorphins when their gazes connected. His heart didn't skip a beat, but it did speed up. His breath didn't catch, but he felt light-headed all the same.

"It might start that way," he said. "That's your body's fight or flight response. But you can choose to run away from it or stick around. When you stick around, the body will find a plateau because that's its natural state. It wants stasis, so that person that initiated those feelings if you both stick around, the feeling will change to something normal."

She'd been eying him skeptically, but there was a slight twitch of her cheek. The twitch pulled down the doubtful brow. It lifted the slight frown. Did part of her want to believe him? Because all of him wanted her to.

"Where are we headed?" she asked.

"I figured since I ruined your taco, I owe you one."

"It wasn't my taco. It was my boss, Mary's taco."

"Your boss? What exactly is it that you do?"

"I work at the library."

Mary? The library? Where he was speaking tomorrow.

Did Elaine know who he was? No, he didn't think she did. Especially not with how she had reacted to him since their first meeting. He didn't have any pictures on his author profile. At first, because he needed to keep his anonymity as he was still in the service. But now that he was out, his publishers were pushing him to do more signings.

"We have a big day there tomorrow," Elaine continued. "Some hack author is coming to do signings."

CHAPTER TEN

He was making a good argument. But he wasn't raising his voice. So, was it an actual argument? What Luke had described between his parents sounded far different than what she'd experienced with her parents.

Gentleness. Kindness. Consideration.

Elaine preferred her parents apart than together. Their simpering anger was better than their wild passion. In any case, she didn't want to talk about love or passion anymore.

Luke had been guiding her, walking on the outside of the street. Actually, crossing over to the outside of the street each time they turned a corner. Seems he was determined if a car should hop the curb, it would hit him first. He was taking this hero thing a little too far. But she didn't say anything about it. She kept in step with him between her neighbor's picket fences and his strong shoulders.

He'd gone silent as they came up to the restaurant. He pulled the door of Castro's Mexican Cuisine open. Juan stopped in his tracks when he saw them.

"It's not a date," Elaine said as Juan tossed their menus on the table. "He's thanking me for saving his life."

Juan still gave Luke the stank eye as he took his order. Elaine winced when Luke asked for a substitution. Juan was usually annoyed at any alteration to his menu.

"I'm worried there might be a sneeze in your burrito," said Elaine, trying for the brevity they'd shared on the way here. But Luke seemed distracted. "Juan and I have never dated, in case you're wondering."

Luke turned back to her. She noted his body posture was rigid. He was sucking in his cheeks, as though he was trying to hold his tongue. His body was turned at an angle, as though he were shielding himself from her. Elaine realized she preferred his open chest from when he walked on the outside of the sidewalk.

"I've never dated anyone," she clarified. "Not that I wasn't asked. I just—"

"You don't believe in love."

Elaine nodded, but her head felt light like it was disconnected from her neck. Her hands fidgeted, and she wished she was holding a book. But she hadn't brought one with her tonight.

"You also don't appear to appreciate any literature that was written in the twenty-first century." He speared a tortilla chip into the bowl of salsa.

"What's that supposed to mean? I'm a librarian. Of course, I love books. You have something against libraries?"

"No, they are one of my favorite places in the world."

"Mine, too. I spent many an after school day there."

"Because of your parents?"

Why had she told him about her parents? Now, he'd think of her as some wounded animal. Which she was not.

She decided to change the subject. "Hey, what book were you reading when I saved your life?"

"The first Walker Skye book."

"Oh," she sighed. Her heart rate slowed. Her

blood flow evened out until it was closer to still waters. Had he said a classic, any classic, it might have skipped a beat.

"Oh?" He leaned forward. Not quite crowding her space, but definitely crossing the line.

Elaine shrugged, not wanting to disparage the author like she promised Mary. Here was one of his fans, and Mr. Skye was coming to the library to talk. She might as well invite Luke to meet him. "He's doing a signing at the library tomorrow. You should come to meet him."

"I think I will come," he said. "But you don't seem excited to meet him."

"Military Science Fiction is not my cup of tea."

"Right, you're a Hardy girl."

"Hardy wrote important works about struggle and morality and the futility of love." She didn't mean to jump back on that subject. But here they were again.

"Futile is definitely a word I'd use to describe those books," said Luke. "There's no justice for Tess. She pays a hefty price because of what others did to her."

Now Elaine leaned forward, stepping over into Luke's territory. "No, it shows that if you succumb to passion, you will suffer."

"I think we read two entirely different books. I read a book where an abused woman finds love. But that love casts her off because of what someone else did to her. If you love someone, you're there through thick and thin. It says so in the vows."

"Not everyone keeps their promises." Elaine broke a tortilla chip in half and crumpled the pieces into the salsa bowl.

"That's a very sad fact. But it doesn't apply to all people." Luke scooped up the broken bits with a whole chip and plopped it all into his mouth.

She wouldn't hold his gaze. "You think Walker Skye's space war books are better. Those books are entirely unrealistic."

"Again, I disagree," Luke said after a sip of water. "They show the triumph of the human spirit. They show that an underdog can win, especially if he or she is backed by a support system. It shows that every person has value. At least that's what I get out of them."

"You're very passionate about these books."

"I read *Tess of the d'Ubervilles* and am making an informed comparison. I think you should give Walker Skye a try. To be fair."

Elaine brushed the crumbs and residual oil of the chips off her hands. "I suppose I should read a few chapters since the author is coming to my place of business."

Juan arrived then with their burritos. Luke offered the cook a smile, which was not returned. They ate in companionable silence. Luke steered the conversation away from love and books. He told her instead about his time in the military. He asked her questions about the town and its people. He listened more than he talked. He leaned forward, asking for details. If the military didn't work out, he might have a career in small-town journalism or detective work with the way he paid attention.

When the check came, Elaine reached for it. He held up his hands as if in defeat. His grin caught her off guard.

"No argument?" she said.

"I'm secure enough in my masculinity to have a woman pay for a five-dollar burrito." Luke waggled his eyebrows.

Elaine had to fight back a smile at the facial expression. She was finding it endearing.

"It was actually seven because you got extra guacamole." She counted out the cash, including a sizable tip for Juan for showing a modicum of civility.

"Looks like I'm a cheap date." Luke held up his hands. "Oops, sorry. Not a date."

"Right." But the word felt thick as guacamole on Elaine's tongue.

Luke offered her his arm as they walked out. "This is a gentlemanly gesture," he said when she hesitated. "It was very popular in the Victorian age."

Instead of arguing, Elaine found herself taking Luke's arm. They walked in silence for a few moments; bellies full, safe topics exhausted. The silence was easy. She liked the warmth of his body. The strength of his forearm. The certainty of his stride. And then she was being crushed against his body.

The dinging bell of a cyclist whizzed in her ear. Her nose was crushed into the side of Luke's neck. She got a strong whiff of aftershave, cilantro, and male. Her belly grumbled as though it was nowhere near full and was hankering for a large helping of dessert.

"I saved your life that time," he said.

"So, we're even?" she asked, her voice breathy as she gazed up at him.

The way he smiled at her made her take another whiff of him. She felt her blood flow increase and pool in her fingertips and cheeks. Her heart didn't skip a beat, but she became acutely aware of its pounding.

"Yes," he said.

His gaze was on her lips. His hands held her elbows. There was an inch between them, but she could still feel his heart.

"We're even," he said.

Disappointment washed through her, causing her to shiver. What reason would they have to see each other again now?

"You cold?" Luke pulled his jacket off.

Elaine ducked away from the romantic gesture. The last thing she needed was to have his scent embedded in her clothes. "Just tired. I think I need to lie down."

"Of course." Concern shone through his gaze. "Let's get you home."

He slipped back into his jacket and wrapped an arm around her waist. She knew the arm was to support her, though she didn't need it. Still, she didn't shrug it off.

Elaine couldn't remember the last time she'd been held, hugged. She felt Luke's pulse thrumming as his hand rested on her hip. She felt his heart beating where her shoulder met his chest. For a moment, her world tuned to the sounds of another.

She walked to his rhythm all the way to her house, her safe haven. They climbed the steps together. There was still some dirt from the spilled pot. But the plant was fine, not wilting at all.

Elaine turned to Luke at the top of the stair. He had stepped down a rung. So they were eye level.

"Tonight was fun," he said.

"You argue literature with all your friends?"

"No, most of my friends prefer hack military science fiction to literature," he said the word *literature* with a snotty accent.

Elaine felt like a snob. She wished she'd behaved better. That she'd kept some of her opinions to herself. She didn't want him thinking badly about her.

Because they were going to be friends.

Should she invite him inside for coffee? No, that's what someone on a date would do. What would a friend do?

"I'll see you tomorrow," Luke said, stepping down one stair.

"Tomorrow?"

"For the signing with the hack author." There was a bite behind his smile.

"He's probably not a hack," Elaine admitted.

"Hang on a second." Luke ran to his truck. He

was back in a moment with a book. "See for yourself."

It was a copy of Walker Skye's first book. "So, now I have homework."

"That's how dinner with friends ends. Had this been a date, there might have been a kiss."

She held his gaze this time. Sweat collected in the palm of her hands. Her fingertips tingled with the need to touch. And then his hand was between them.

"Goodnight, Elaine."

Elaine put her hand in his. Her palms were clammy. His were damp too. But there was heat between them. That heat evaporated the droplets.

Luke took the last few steps down the stairs and hopped in his truck. Elaine stayed for a few moments on the front steps, holding the book to her chest. Then she cracked open the cover.

CHAPTER ELEVEN

"You know that was a sign, right?"

Luke turned to Paul, but only for a second. He had to keep his eyes on the road. Not only did he need to worry about other cars, but he also needed to worry about pedestrians. Most were looking down at their phones and not flipping through a book.

"What are you talking about?" said Luke.

"That lingering handshake? Totally a sign that she wanted you to kiss her."

"It was not." Was it? "She did not." Did she? "It wasn't a date. Therefore, there were no signs."

Except maybe there were signs. When Luke had thought Elaine was cold and he'd gone to do the gentlemanly thing with his jacket, she'd stepped back. But she hadn't shrugged him off when he put his arm around her as they walked. In fact, she kinda burrowed herself into his side like he was a favorite pillow.

They had been silent as they walked. But it wasn't uncomfortable. It was pleasant. They'd said everything they had to say back at the restaurant, and man had they said a lot.

Then there was that handshake. Luke had certainly felt sparks. Perhaps, she had too. He'd heard her gasp, only because he'd been paying such close attention to everything about her.

Her lips had parted. Her gaze had dipped. Had they dipped to his lips? He wasn't sure. He couldn't take his eyes off her at the time to determine where she was looking.

Had it been a sign?

Luke was normally a good read of people. He had to be in his former line of work in the armed services. But it truly served him in his current line of work as a novelist.

Writing wasn't just about plot. It was about character growth and development. That's what truly got his readers hooked; that he could get to the heart of what his heroine, and even the villain, wanted. What motivated them to go after a goal.

Which conflicts he could put in their path to test them and get them to grow. That's what got him five-star reviews.

But Luke couldn't read Elaine. She was a walking, talking, reading contradiction. He knew he'd scare her off if he pushed. But man did he want to push. He just didn't want her running scared before he could pull her in.

"You might be right," Luke admitted.

"I know I'm right," snorted Paul. "I know women."

"Not this one. She's afraid of emotions. Her parents' love story sounded warped."

Luke told Paul what Elaine had told him about her parents' divorces and remarriages. He could fill in the blanks that the Reynolds's passion was destructive. He'd seen the end product in their daughter.

"That's interesting," said Paul. "Your parents' love story is on the other end of that spectrum."

"What am I gonna do?"

"Why do you even like this girl?" asked Paul.

Good question. "She's beautiful. She's smart."

All surface-level observations.

"She's opinionated," he went on.

Which might turn off another man, but he liked the challenge.

"She's a strong woman," he continued.

She had to be after what her parents had put her through as a child. She'd come through the other end scarred, wounded. Like a soldier after a war. But like Luke, Elaine didn't have a visible scratch on her. All her hurts were on the inside.

"There's a softness to her. Something in her eyes that tells me she needs to be held."

"Another rescue," sighed Paul.

"What are you talking about?"

"It's clear as the plot of one of your books," said his friend. "You feel like you need to rescue everyone."

Luke opened his mouth to argue. Then closed it. Most of his relationships had been with women in the service. There were no wilting flowers there.

He had fallen for Jessica Kilmeade while she was in the infirmary. He'd started dating Tonya Horwitz after she was medically discharged, but that only lasted until she was on the mend.

He'd noticed Elaine when she was reading while eating a taco. But he'd felt that spark of something when she'd been lying unconscious in a hospital bed. Was he a rescue romantic?

"Wait?" said Paul. "You said she works at the library?"

"Yes," Luke said, parking in a visitor spot at said library. It was one of the last. When he'd come here the other day, he'd had his pick of spots.

"Did you tell her who you are?"

"Nope. She called Walker Skye a hack. Even though she's never read my books. I gave her a copy last night."

"This is gonna be good." Paul chuckled. "Better than watching a telenovela."

"I don't understand why you watch those. You don't even speak Spanish."

"Drama is clear in every language."

Paul hopped out of the car and winced. Luke held his tongue as his friend massaged his low back. He knew better than to notice Paul's pain.

The familiar pang of guilt washed over him. Then the guilt washed out of him when he spotted Elaine. She was behind the circulation desk. His book was in her hands. Anxiety took up the space where guilt fled.

"That her?" asked Paul.

Luke couldn't answer. He was too busy watching as Elaine's eyes scanned across the pages. She wasn't smiling. She wasn't frowning. Was that a thoughtful look? Did she hate it? Had she found a grammatical error? A plot hole?

"You said her favorite book is *Tess of the d'Urbervilles*?" asked Paul.

Luke wanted to shush the man like they were in a movie theater, and the opening credits were through. Paul was talking at the opening, pivotal scene that would set up the whole story. "I don't know if it's her favorite."

"A book where secrets destroy the life of the heroine?"

Luke had never noticed that theme. But, then again, he hadn't thought about the book much since the one time he'd had to read and write a paper about it in school.

"You are doomed, my friend," Paul said with glee, clapping Luke on the shoulder.

"Mr. Skye, we're so happy you're here." Mary, the librarian, was dressed more like a naughty librarian today. Her skirt was so tight her knees stayed pressed together as she walked. Her blouse had one too many buttons undone. Her make up could be seen from miles away.

"You have a full house awaiting your reading," said Mary. "We'll be ready in just a moment."

"Thank you, Ms. Charles. Everything looks great."

"Oh, no need to be so formal," she leaned in.

"Please, call me Mary. I thought we might grab dinner afterward to celebrate—"

"Would you excuse me for just one moment?" asked Luke.

He walked away from the head librarian to the assistant at the circulation desk. Elaine didn't look up at his approach. Her nose was buried in his book. Was that a good sign? Maybe she was enjoying it. He had to find out.

"What do you think?" he asked.

Elaine looked up. It took a second before recognition dawned. Her expression changed from pensive to pleased. Luke felt something turn over inside him.

Elaine offered him a little smile as she reached for a cloth bookmark and put it in-between the pages. Luke felt a bit disappointed that she didn't dog-ear the page and leave a permanent imprint on his work.

"It's not bad," she said. "It's not Pulitzer material either. The writing flows. The descriptions aren't flowery, but they're evocative."

Luke's chest puffed up at all the compliments. He was ready to come clean that it was his pen that had written those flowing, evocative words.

"It's just that the relationships are unbelievable. I

can't believe that these people would get behind an untried leader so quickly and believe in her so thoroughly."

It wasn't quite a slap in the face. It did shake off the puffy feelings in his chest.

"That's what happens when someone saves your life," Paul spoke from behind Luke. "In the book, the captain saved their lives, and now she feels a sense of loyalty to them and they to her. You ever notice that?"

Paul looked pointedly at Luke. Luke glanced at Paul. Elaine glanced between the two, clearly waiting patiently for an introduction to the newcomer.

"This is my friend, Major Paul Hanson," said Luke.

"Did you save Lieutenant Jackson's life, Major Hanson?"

"Not me," said Paul. "The lieutenant here is the hero. He threw his body on mine to protect me from a grenade," said Paul.

"That happen a lot around you?" Elaine asked Luke. "What is it? Do you attract danger?"

"No, I'm a regular guy," said Luke.

"Excuse me, Mr. Skye?"

Luke had heard many an explosion go off in his

career in the military. Those four words were louder than a bomb.

"Can I get your autograph?" The woman held his two books to her ample bosom. Luke wasn't sure where to reach. Especially when the only thing he wanted to reach out to was Elaine.

Elaine's brow crinkled. Then realization dawned. He only saw it because he watched her so closely, but he was sure he saw her gaze shutter closed.

CHAPTER TWELVE

It always came down to secrets.

Elaine looked from the man she thought she was getting to know and down to the cover of the book she had been getting into. She was surprised she had been enjoying the bit of pulp fiction. There were thousands of words written on the page. But Luke had forgotten to tell her the most important ones. There were only two that mattered; that he was Walker Skye.

With one final glance at her, Luke took his place at the lectern. He'd lied to her.

Well, he hadn't stood in front of her and told her a bald-faced lie. But omission was just as strong. That's what her parents' fights had taught her.

Elaine wasn't sure if the two of them had ever cheated on one another. She doubted it. Who else would put up with the madness they inflicted on each other. She was their daughter, and she didn't want to deal with it.

But they'd kept secrets. They'd said hurtful things. Then the next hour, the next day, the next week, they'd take it back. Only to repeat the cycle the next month.

They never tired of fussing and fighting. They could cut each other so deep, not recognizing the collateral damage it did to those around them. Because just as much as they salted the wounds, they were also the salve. It was a sickness Elaine did not want to allow into her system.

Luke looked away from her. Before he turned, Elaine saw remorse was clear on his face. He hadn't tried to make amends with her. He hadn't tried to explain. He'd taken the buxom woman's book and signed; Walker Skye. There was a flourish with the Y in his last name. Or his fake last name.

Or maybe that was his real name. Elaine had no clue.

He walked up to the lectern, where his books were placed on display. It was a packed house, more people than had visited the library all week. He didn't glance at her when he spoke. His gaze remained cast down.

"I'm supposed to do a reading from my book, but I'd like to tell you a story you might not know instead."

Luke looked up then and found her gaze across the crowded room. But Elaine couldn't hold his gaze. How could she when she could no longer trust his words; the ones he spoke as well as what he'd written.

"I felt powerless as a child," he said. "My mother died because of me."

Gasps went around the audience. The audience was a good mix of men and women. But where the men were dressed in casual slacks and jeans, all of the women wore tight clothes and a pound of makeup.

Elaine had never seen half of them in the library. They were all here for the famous Walker Skye. The man who wrote strong female protagonists that led armies to defeat evil empires. Yet, here, her creator was peddling lies.

But wait? Hadn't he told her this the other night?

"My father always told me that it wasn't my fault.

I even have letters where my mother tells me that her death wasn't my fault. She knew the risks going into the pregnancy. But she wanted to take the chance. In her letters, she told me I was worth it."

Every person was riveted to his words. Including Elaine. Something in her told her he was telling the truth.

"Every heroine I write is my mother. The woman I met in the letters. The woman that believes that everyone deserves a chance, even if it means that she doesn't make it in the end."

Elaine's anger was dying down. She had the urge to reach out to him. To grab his wrist and tug him out of danger. To take off her cardigan and wrap it around his shoulders.

Last night, Luke hadn't told her this part of the story. But why would he? She had disparaged his books before he could even say anything.

"I joined the military not only to do my part for this country that has provided so many opportunities. I did it because, well, I wanted to be someone's hero."

He wasn't looking at her, but Elaine felt his attention on her. She knew this information was more for her ears than his fans. Was this his apology?

"The reality of war is a harsh one. Both at home and on the war front. It's not always clean boots and pristine outfits. There's sweat. There's dirt. There's blood. Writing these stories was how I escaped, but it's also how I planned to make the world better. The military is how societies protect themselves. Science is how we try to understand the world. Fiction is how we dream the world could be."

He did look at her then. This time, Elaine met Luke's gaze. Everyone else in the room disappeared. Gone was the salt she'd felt at his betrayal. His words were more than an apology. They were a salve.

"I put all those together in my books to bring forth a vision of how the world could be a better place. I've seen destruction and death. Military science fiction is more than politics in space. It's also literature that investigates our morality. It forces us to soul search in unfamiliar territory. And hopefully, come out the other end a better species."

There was loud booming applause. Elaine took a moment of refuge in the crowd's boisterous praise. She took a deep breath. She hadn't realized she'd been holding her breath as Luke spoke. She'd hung on his every word. Much like she'd hung on every word of his book, so far.

True, Elaine didn't suspend her disbelief at the

character of the captain and her plight. But Elaine had wanted to believe in her.

"Samuel Langhorne Clemens."

Elaine turned back to Major Hanson. "I beg your pardon?

"Mark Twain's pen name," he clarified. "Mary Ann Evans was better known as George Eliot. Charles Lutwidge Dodgson is known to most as Lewis Carroll. And we can't forget Eric Arthur Blair, better known as George Orwell. They all had pen names for various reasons. Luke started writing while we were still in the service. Some plots hit close to the battlefield, and he would've gotten in serious trouble if our superiors knew what he was doing. He's retired now and coming out of the pen box for the first time."

Elaine plopped down in the chair behind the circulation desk. Her legs felt worn out like she'd ran a marathon. Her arms felt sore like she'd been on both sides of the rope in a tug of war.

"He likes you," said Major Hanson. "More than friends. I know because the pen keeps slipping from his hands up there. His palms sweat when he likes a woman."

Elaine looked up as Luke was listening to

someone ask a question. Sure enough, the pen he held slipped from his fingers. His palms had been sweaty the other night when they'd said their goodbyes. So had hers.

Instead of admitting that, or addressing any of the facts Major Hanson stated, Elaine said, "That's a long line of women there."

"They're here for Walker Skye. You came for Luke Jackson."

"We're just friends," Elaine insisted.

"I don't think so."

Major Hanson's shoulders were back, his chest out, and his chin high. His confidence irked Elaine.

"Walker?" called a woman from the audience. Her lipstick was so red, Elaine wondered if she wasn't bleeding. "Your heroine is such a strong character. Will she never find love?"

The pen slipped through Luke's fingers again. He left it on the lectern this time. "My parents had the greatest love story I know. So, I've only seen a man loving a ghost."

"I have a follow-up," said the blood-lipped woman. "What do you look for in a woman?"

Luke swallowed before he answered. He reached for the pen, then must've thought better of it because he put his hand behind his back. "Well-read. Open-minded. Believes in love."

Two out of three. Or maybe one out of three. Well, that wasn't Elaine. Which proved he wasn't truly interested in her. Not that it mattered. They were just friends.

Luke stepped down from the lectern and was immediately mobbed by the women. But he moved for the younger people with books to sign.

"He is even yummier in person," said Mary. "I thought he would be the broody type. Collecting numbers and waxing poetic about his time in the service to get the women to swoon over him.“

"He's not like that at all," said Elaine.

"How would you know?" said Mary.

"They went on a date last night," said Major Hanson.

"It was not a date," said Elaine.

"Him?" said Mary. “That was your soldier?"

"He's not my soldier," said Elaine.

"Elaine, why didn't you call dibs?” Mary threw up her hands. “I wore my best bra for him today. This thing pinches ... "

"He's fair game,” Elaine insisted. “You know I don't date."

"Right," said Mary, glancing between Elaine and

Luke. "You're clearly not interested in him. And he's clearly not interested in you."

Luke glanced up at her every other book he signed. As she moved through the library, she felt his gaze on her. She watched as every single woman came up to him. It was clear they were flirting. But, time after time, he shook his head or turned down a card or written note. And then his gaze would find her again.

Elaine felt the butterflies in her stomach. She could hear her pulse thumping. Despite many deep breaths, she couldn't help her heart racing and her mind wondering.

Everyone in the room knew his stories. But Luke had given her the truth of himself, of his private pain.

"I'm no Angel," Luke said ninety minutes later after the crowd dispersed, and the doors to the library were closed.

The reference to *Tess* was so unexpected that Elaine laughed. Look at her. Laughing at a tragedy.

"Let me explain?" he said.

"You don't have to," said Elaine. "Paul explained. You were protecting yourself. I get it."

Did she? Something like this would've sent her

parents into a tizzy. Surprise was evident on Luke's face. The sparkles danced in his brown eyes.

"So, we can still be friends?" he asked.

Friends. That word felt like a lie

"Yeah." She offered her hand. "Friends."

And there it was again; the tingle.

CHAPTER THIRTEEN

*L*uke's fingers flew across the keyboard. His heroine had just finished a moving speech.

It was right before a pivotal battle scene. His heroine excelled at these because they were her creator's favorite thing to write.

Luke loved movies where the coach rallied the team before the homecoming game. He loved the war movie where the commander gave a moving speech before the big battle.

That swell of emotions. That charge to advance forward and conquer. Luke couldn't get enough of it.

He wasn't at the end of the book. Not yet. In this part of the plot, the Captain and her ragtag team were going to make a small advance on the enemy. Her troops were rallied and ready. She'd thought of every eventuality, and Luke had put each event down on the page as an inner monologue.

All except one. The one eventuality that he'd laid as a trap to trip her up right before the climax of the book. He knew his readers would be flying over the pages at this part of the story. Their anxiety high and their anticipation at an edge.

He'd finished the captain's moving speech. It was one of his best so far. He knew it would move readers. But now, he was stuck.

Luke knew he couldn't have the troops rush directly into battle immediately after the speech. The readers needed a breather scene, a bit of space to digest what was just said, to build the anticipation of what was to come. But what plot device could he use to fill the next few pages before the deciding battle?

Even as he asked himself the question, his fingers began typing. Her second in command, who was a hero in his own right, came into her makeshift office. The man she'd trusted most, the man who knew her best, had a bone to pick with her about her speech.

On one page, they were arguing about the battle plan. On the next page, he had pulled her into his arms and was professing his long-held feelings for her.

Luke's hands froze over the keyboard. His fingers curled away from the keys. The captain remained trapped at the cursor in her best friend's arms. Both his heroine and her author were stunned at this new revelation.

Luke had never intended to go in this direction. He wasn't a romance author. Love stories were not his forte as an author. Or even as a man. He never thought he'd live up to his parents' epic love story. So, he never attempted to write one for himself. Yet, here, love was showing up on the page.

He fought a war with his fingers as they flexed and relaxed. His index fingers twitched to get back to the keys. But his thumbs rested on the space bar. In the end, Luke left the tug of war at a stalemate and backed away from the computer.

He needed some space to work out this particular plot point. Did he want to go down this road with these two? He wasn't sure? He wasn't sure about anything. He needed to take a walk to clear his head.

The good thing about staying on a ranch was there was plenty of space for him to clear his head. And he didn't have to do it on his own two feet.

Luke made it to the stables when the sun was the highest in the sky. He mounted a horse and took off. Horseback riding was like flying. But in this case, he felt both the wind and the power of the ground at the same time.

His head felt clear when he came back to the stables. But he still didn't have an answer to his plot problems.

"Writer's block?"

He turned to find Dr. Patel.

"No," Luke confessed, "the opposite. The book wants to go in a new direction."

"And you don't want it to go that way?"

The man's voice and smile reminded Luke of his own father. So, he couldn't help spilling his guts about his literary problems.

"I'm not sure what I want. My heroine is fearless in battle because she's used to fighting for others. But she's never fought for herself. I don't know how to make her see that she's worthy of love. That having love in her life might add to her life. That it might strengthen her to stand beside someone instead of in front of them. That love isn't a weakness."

Luke looked into the doctor's bright gaze. Patel's gaze was so clear that Luke felt he was looking into a mirror at his own reflection. But all the psychologist did was nod.

"Why does your heroine believe that love is a weakness?"

Good question. "I've kept her backstory vague." Luke paused. His mind turned back to the other night for an answer. "But, what if she came from divorce, her parents' divorced, I mean?"

Patel looked at him as though he knew where this new story was coming from.

"Parents teach kids how to love. Children of divorce have seen both sides of love and know that love can hurt and make people vulnerable. They have seen that love is a risk."

"I'd never hurt her," said Luke. He cleared his throat and began again. "My character, I mean. How do I get her to see that? In dialogue, of course. What could the love interest say to her?"

Dr. Patel nodded. "He—your hero—would have to know that communication is key. He should strive to be honest and open with her. Those two things are paramount."

Well, there went strikes one and two. Luke hadn't given Elaine the whole truth when they'd met. But she'd said it was fine back in the library.

"For dialogue, if your heroine gives short

answers like *I'm fine,* you will know she isn't telling the truth. That is not good communication."

"She said that." Luke sighed, rubbing a hand across his forehead.

"Your character?"

Luke bit his lip. He didn't feel the need to answer. He knew his motives were transparent. But Patel kept up the farce, likely for Luke to save face.

"She's not fine," said Patel. "But, you can use that as subtext in your book."

"What can he—the male love interest—do to win her trust?"

"He can show her support. She'll likely have high expectations due to her need for stability and routine. She'll have a fear of abandonment and will need constant reassurances. For her, love is associated with pain. It'll take time for her to believe it otherwise. How long is this book?"

"I'm willing to make it as long as it needs to be for her to believe it."

Patel patted Luke on his shoulder as they walked away from the stables. "I have a feeling it's going to be a bestseller."

CHAPTER FOURTEEN

*E*laine pinched the top of the last page of the book. Her gaze struggled not to skip ahead a few paragraphs to the end. She wanted to savor every last syllable.

She loved this part of the book. The part when she was not quite done and still in the thick of it. It was like that few moments before the morning alarm went off, and she got to snuggle deeper in bed before the day started.

Walker Skye's book had started slow, even though it was fast-paced. Space battles weren't Elaine's thing. Though that was part of the plot, the book had deeper themes. Morality, acceptance, friendship, family.

The book had begun in medias res with the heroine already having a following of troops. But as Elaine read on, she found out why these people followed her. Elaine read the struggles, the triumphs, the setbacks, and small victories that won the captain her loyalty.

There were times Elaine had cheered and clenched her fist as the book's heroine advanced. At other times, Elaine's palms pressed to her heart when danger lasted for pages. Luke's words were all for the heart and not the head. Always by the captain's side was her second in command. Elaine had read on as his quiet doubt turned to vocal support for the captain. The stoic soldier never pressed his suit, but it was clear that something was bubbling between the two. Luke had said there was no romance at the reading. Still, Elaine saw it.

By the end of the book, the second in command stood by the captain and pledged his loyalty, his fealty. Elaine realized she'd been hoping the soldier would embrace his leader. But that wasn't this kind of story. On the last page, the story ended on a note of hope and anticipation.

Elaine closed the covers and felt a deep sense of satisfaction. The good guys had triumphed and came out stronger. A semblance of balance was restored, and a greater challenge was on the horizon. But the captain, who had been abandoned on the first page of the story, was no longer alone.

Elaine stared at the last three words. She was used to books ending with two words; The End. This book said; To Be Continued …

Elaine couldn't take her gaze off the ellipsis. There was more to this story. She could find out what happened next.

If she wanted to.

She'd never been a fan of series. Standalones were her thing; one and done. But now …

Elaine jerked back as her phone beeped. She dropped the book as though guilty that the caller could read her intentions. She looked over to see Luke's name on the caller ID. She'd given him her cell phone number the other day.

Thank you for inviting me into your world.

Inviting him into her world? It was his book she had devoured.

I had a great time at the library and speaking to your patrons.

Oh. Now she understood. What should she text him back? Should she text him back? Looking down at her phone, she saw the ellipsis was bubbling on his end. He wasn't done. There was more he had to say.

I look forward to Sunday dinner at the ranch.

The ellipsis stopped, and the ball, or rather the cursor, was in her court. But she still didn't know what to say. She didn't like text conversations, not even with Mary. Elaine preferred to speak in person. So, she decided, she'd just wait for that time to speak to Luke.

Elaine began her routine. She dressed for work. She walked to the library. She unlocked the door and turned on the lights and computers.

The display of classic books and literature was at the front of the room. But in a stand next to it were Walker Skye's Book One and Book Two.

Elaine reached for Book Two. She looked around the empty library before opening the cover. She read the first passage, intending only to see where the book was headed. She was immediately sucked into the continuing tale. So much so, that she didn't hear the door open.

"Just friends, huh?" Elaine looked up to see Mary standing over her with a raised brow, a smug grin, and three Harlequins in hand.

"It's a professional courtesy that I read his book," said Elaine.

"That's book two, meaning you finished book one last night. And you must've liked it."

"He's really good," Elaine admitted. "He makes you want to believe in ... possibilities.

Mary set the Harlequins down. She reached across the desk and grabbed Elaine's hands in her own. "You deserve a possibility, Elaine."

Elaine's fingers trembled as Mary squeezed. But she didn't pull away. She held on.

"That man had half the eligible women in the town fawning over him," Mary continued. "He only had eyes for you."

Before Elaine could respond, the bell dinged over the library announcing new patrons. In walked their two regulars for the last few weeks. Two college students from the local university who had been paired as partners for a literary project.

"We are not putting that in our paper," said the female in a knee-length skirt and cardigan. The girl could've come straight out of Elaine's closet. "It has nothing to do with *Tess of the d'Urbervilles.*"

And Elaine's bookshelf, apparently.

The young man behind her was dressed in rugged jeans and a button-up. His hair was buzz-cut as though he'd been in the military, though he looked too young.

"In Tess, Hardy says your history determines your future, and you don't have control over it. But Skye's heroine took control and overcame her past, instead of continuing to suffer. She doesn't run away. She faces her demons and wins."

"Against aliens in space," countered Elaine's double.

If Elaine hadn't been certain before, there was confirmation they were talking about Luke's books.

"It's not about the space battle," said the young man. "Just like Tess isn't about the d'Urberville name. It's internally who you are and how you present yourself to the world."

"He's right," said Elaine. All gazes turned to her. She would've turned a shocked glance on herself had she been anyone but herself. "You can't let how others behaved in the past rewrite your whole life. Tess should've fought back. She should've fought Alec. She should've spoken up to Angel."

"Now you're talking," said Mary.

She was talking. And she didn't want to stop talking. She pulled out her phone but knew a text message wouldn't do.

"I have to go," said Elaine.

"Don't you dare come back without a Jedi Knight," Mary called after her.

Elaine grabbed her cardigan and the book.

"Wait," said Mary. "You do have to check out that book before you take it. We're librarians, not heathens."

CHAPTER FIFTEEN

"How's it going with the librarian?" asked Maggie.

She sat in a rocking chair on someone's porch. Luke was fairly certain it wasn't her house. But that's how people came and went on this ranch.

Luke and Paul had been headed back to their place. Luke had waited outside the doctor's offices where Paul got results from his tests. He'd had been waiting patiently for his friend to tell him what the doctor said, but Paul kept skirting the subject. Now, they were on a subject Luke wanted to skirt.

Luke tried not to sigh, but with another glance of his phone and his unanswered text message, the weary gush of air came out. "She said she's coming over for Sunday dinner."

Well, she had said that when he'd seen her last. She hadn't responded to any of his texts today. Luke's fingers itched to text again, but he knew he was pushing it.

"You're at the meet the family stage already?" Maggie cuddled the baby, who slept on her chest. Again, Luke didn't think this was her child. But again, that's how the people and kids on this ranch came and went. "That's progressing nicely."

"I expect a proposal in less than a month," said another of the brides. Cassie Ramos poked her head out of the screen door. Luke thought she might be the child's mother?

"It's not like that between me and Elaine," said Luke. "We're still just friends."

"Yeah," said Maggie. "The way you said that isn't believable."

Luke sighed again. "She spooks easy. I need to take it slow. Get her comfortable."

"You make her sound like a new colt," said Cassie.

She was. Elaine hadn't responded to any of his text messages. Maybe Dr. Patel had it wrong. Maybe he was coming on too strong and scaring her off?

"These women will have you married by three months if you're not careful," said Paul.

That didn't sound so bad to Luke. He could see himself discussing books with Elaine over tacos on Tuesdays for weeks, months, to come. Maybe even years.

"Wow? Really?" said Paul as he eyed his best friend. "What do you even know about this girl?"

"That's just it," said Luke. "I'm trying to get to know her."

"What you're trying to do is save her," said Paul.

"She saved me," Luke insisted.

"I've seen her. She's a wounded bird. She's hurt on the inside. You told me her parents made a mess of the nest and flew the coop. Now, here you come to save her. Not every wound is your fault. Not every scrape needs healing."

The longer Paul spoke, the touchier his tone got. Luke knew his friend, and he wasn't taking the bait. This wasn't about him and Elaine. "What did the doctor say?"

Paul looked away from Luke. Over in the neighboring yard, a few of the men played football. "I'm not getting surgery. I'm fine. I'm leaving here and going back home at the end of the week."

"Paul—"

"You can stay and court the librarian if you want, but don't use me as an excuse."

"If the doctor—"

"It's my life. It's my decision. My condition is a manageable one. This is how I choose to manage it."

The football landed between them as though to punctuate the end of the argument. Paul picked up the pigskin and tossed it back. He winced with the throw.

"Good arm," called Xavier Ramos.

"It's been a minute," said Paul

"Come play," Ramos invited.

Paul hesitated for a second before joining the other guys. Luke held back. Instead of joining in the game, he took the opportunity to watch his friend. He searched for any other signs of pain and discomfort. After fifteen minutes, he didn't see any. He only saw joy on Paul's face at the normal interaction between other fit men. Maybe his friend was okay?

The crunch of gravel turned Luke's attention from the game and to the road. A car pulled up. When the vehicle came to a stop, Elaine hopped out. She was holding Luke's book in her hand. Luke rose from his chair. As she approached, he saw that it wasn't the book he'd given her. It was the second one.

"I finished the first and started the second," she

said, her voice breathless, her words were stilted as though she had difficulty forming them. "I really like it."

A slow grin spread across Luke's face. "You sound surprised."

"Because I didn't expect to. I prejudged the book and the author. But last night, I gave the story a try." She hesitated. Her brow pinching. Her lips contorting. "And I really liked it."

"I'm glad you like it. I'm partial to it myself."

"Maybe we could discuss it … over tacos?"

"I'd like that."

Elaine bit her lip, as though chewing on her next words. "Maybe not as friends. Maybe as two people who...like each other."

Luke knew he should take it slow. He knew she was spookable. But he had no trouble getting his words out. "Do you mean a date?"

Elaine nodded.

"I'd really like that."

Behind them were a few girlish squeals of delight. They turned to see Maggie and Cassie applauding the scene that he'd just played out.

"I love this place," sighed Maggie as the baby in her arms burped and deposited a little gift on her pristine blouse.

CHAPTER SIXTEEN

"So, how did you two meet again?"

Elaine sat in the dining room of Beth Barrett's house. Although she supposed she was Beth Cartwright now having married Reece Cartwright.

Elaine was surrounded by other familiar faces from her past. She'd gone to school with Maggie Banks, Eva DeMonti, and Ginger Chase as well. Though none of them had run in the same circles. Elaine hadn't had a circle. Her nose was always in a book.

But she'd had classes with Maggie. She'd seen Beth in church. And she'd been lab partners with Eva once. Now, these girls were all one big clique. It boggled the mind.

"Luke was about to get hit by a car," said Elaine. "And I kinda saved him."

"Well, that's one for the books," said Eva.

Elaine looked about the room at the nods of approval. "One what?"

"Meet cute," said Ginger.

"What's a meet-cute?" asked Elaine.

Maggie set a glass of homemade lemonade down on the table in front of Elaine. "It's a romance novel term for when the two love interests meet."

Love interests? Elaine should've shuddered at that. But she didn't.

"Beth and Reece re-met when Reece lost his memory," Maggie continued. "Amnesia trope. Brandon heard Reegan sing, and he fell in love. Fran rescued Eva from prepubescent gangsters. And my dogs brought Dylan and me together."

Elaine's head spun at the many and varied and unbelievable pairings.

"But, I think you're our first actual heroine to save the soldier," said Maggie.

"Oh," said Elaine, holding up her hands. "This isn't the start of a ..."

The three women all looked at her with raised eyebrows. Their triplet smiles stopped Elaine's mouth from moving. Leaving her sentence hanging on an ellipsis to be continued.

Was she ready for an ellipsis? Would she continue this story with a romance? Elaine gulped when she realized her answer.

"It's gonna be my first date," Elaine admitted.

The women clapped and cooed. Elaine did not feel elated. Panic set in.

Should she even start this? What if it didn't turn out well? What if it turned into something more? Was he even here permanently?Would he move in? Would he expect her to move out? What if he wanted to mix their bookshelves?

"Leave her alone," said Dylan Banks as he walked into the door with his toddler in hand. "Not every date needs to end in marriage."

Maggie rounded on her husband. "Says the man who asked me to marry him the day we met."

Dylan ignored his wife's fact and handed over the child. "Can you take him? I'm gonna go play ball with the guys."

"I'm having girl-time here," Maggie countered.

Dylan looked around the room. "It looks to me like you're pressuring someone to join your squad."

"My squad?"

Elaine's shoulders hunched as Maggie's brows

rose. Like a bloodhound, Elaine smelled a fight brewing. With that knowledge, panic left her, and anxiety settled in. She wanted to be anywhere but here with two parents fighting.

Elaine looked at the little boy. He looked back and forth between his parents. But instead of crying or even frowning, the child was giggling.

Elaine hated that his innocence would soon be lost when he came to understand the insults and the hurts being flung over his head by the people who were supposed to care about him the most. But the child was still oblivious. For now.

Elaine turned away from the couple to Beth, Ginger, and Eva. The other women didn't look away from the fight. They leaned in, shoveling snacks into their mouths and sipping their lemonade.

"Yeah," said Dylan. "Squad. I know I use that word right. I heard the kids say it."

"We are totally a squad," said Maggie, poking a finger into her husband's chest. "And we have squad goals. We aim to increase our ranks until every woman in Montana is as deliriously happy as we all are."

Maggie tilted her head back. Dylan ducked down and kissed her. Their son giggled. Elaine stared between the three.

"But you're keeping the kid for another thirty minutes," said Maggie when she pulled away from the kiss.

Dylan groaned. But there was no bite to it. He didn't even look put out that he'd lost the fight. He lifted his son into his arms like he was a football. "Fine. I'll catch the ball one-handed."

"Dylan Banks, my son better not come back with any dents."

"I make no promises." Dylan shifted his son into the other arm. The kid dissolved into a fit of giggles. The door closed quietly behind him.

Elaine blinked a couple of times, still unable to accept what she'd just witnessed.

"He's right," said Maggie. "I'm sorry, Elaine. I know not all women want to get married. I just—"

"How did you do that?" said Elaine.

"Do what?"

"You two just fought. And then you made up. Quickly. With no broken dishes. No slammed doors. You barely raised your voices."

"Oh, honey, that wasn't a fight," said Maggie.

She had that right. No one was crying or cursing or packing an overnight bag.

"Marriage isn't always easy," Maggie continued. "Communication is key."

"Preach sister," said Beth. "Add patience and forgiveness to that."

Ginger held up her hand. "I'll toss in humility and trust."

"Top that off with love and commitment," said Eva.

"If you build that in a dating relationship," said Maggie, "you have a good chance of making a good marriage."

Elaine wasn't so sure. Instead of arguing, like she'd been taught by her parents to do, she sat back, sipped her tea, and observed these happily married unicorns and their strange customs.

CHAPTER SEVENTEEN

*L*uke caught the pass and ran it into the makeshift end zone. He threw up his hands in celebration. The men on his team whooped. The dogs running around their feet yipped. But Luke only had eyes for Elaine.

She sat on the porch with the wives and the small children of the ranch. Elaine looked out of place in her cardigan and plaid skirt while the other women were in jeans or sundresses. The wives of the Purple Heart Ranch had their hair loose, flowing freely around their shoulders. Scuffs and dirt were a part of their wardrobe, just like their wedding bands.

They surrounded Elaine. More like ants scenting a sweet treat than anything else. Pretty soon, they'd cart her off through their collective effort and bring them back to their queen. Maggie stood in the doorway, waiting for the addition to her ranks.

Instead of rooting for his touchdown, Luke wanted to root for the hive surrounding Elaine. Slowly, she was loosening up. She didn't look like she belonged here. But she was clearly becoming more comfortable the longer she stayed.

"Eyes on the ball, Romeo."

Luke frowned at Paul. He was more annoyed with the analogy his friend had used than being called out. "Romeo and Juliet ended in tragedy."

Luke certainly did not want his story with Elaine to end in a murder-suicide.

"A tragedy?" said Paul. "Sounds like the exact ending your team is about to experience."

Luke laughed at that. It was good to play and joke with Paul. It was good to see the man's cheeks flush with exertion.

Paul had been cooped up for the last two years. In and out of doctor's visits. On and off bed rest.

Luke didn't miss the winces and grimaces that had become a part of his friend's everyday struggles. Luke had to admit that he was experiencing a few winces and grimaces himself as he played with the other men. He was severely out of practice on the football field for all the writing he'd been doing the last two years.

The soldiers of the Purple Heart Ranch had their fair share of internal and external injuries. But not a single one of them let his injuries keep him down. Reed was a master blocker with his prosthetic arm. Dylan kept pace with all the men with his prosthetic leg.

Their injuries weren't the end of any of them. Luke knew that finding love had played the biggest part in each of their healing. He wondered if he could be so lucky having found Elaine when he wasn't injured.

Not that he was in love with her.

He just liked her.

A lot.

Paul had been wrong about Luke's tendencies with women. There Elaine sat, fit and fine. The bump on her head was gone. She had no bruises, save the ones her parents had left behind. And she was working to heal those wounds. All signs proving that Luke did not have a thing for wounded women.

"Heads up, Jackson."

Luke lifted his head in time to see the ball. It came straight for his nose. He had no time to duck out of its path before it touched down. Right in his face. He went crashing down to the ground.

"I told you, Romeo," came Paul's voice. "Such a tragedy."

Luke rubbed at his nose. He didn't come away with any blood. Just a bruised ego.

"Are you okay?" Elaine was over him.

Luke would've sworn he saw birds flying around her head. Man, he had it bad for this woman. "Yeah, I'm good."

"Are you sure you're okay?"

Elaine's hand cupped Luke's cheek. Her warm touch spread across the entire surface area of his skin. He wasn't okay. He was in desperate need, in desperate need of his lips on hers.

"You tackled me harder than that ball," he said.

There was a double meaning in his words. He was sure Elaine got them by the blush on her cheek.

"Why don't you go walk it off," said Dylan.

Luke came to his feet. Elaine kept a hand around his forearm like he'd done to her the night of their thank-you dinner. Like she was the gentleman in Victorian England. He didn't need her assistance, but he liked having it. He liked having her on his arm.

They walked away from the game. Away from

the prying eyes of the soldiers and the busybody-
ness of their wives.

Luke took Elaine over to the house he shared
with Paul. The place wasn't much lived in. Which
reminded him, if Paul was going to leave, then Luke
didn't have much reason to stay. Except he had every
reason to stay.

Elaine grabbed an ice cube from the tray in the
freezer. Then, turning back to him, she pressed the
cube to his cheek. The solid quickly turned to liquid
with the heat between them.

"Paul's treatment is going to be up sooner than
we thought."

The cube slipped from Elaine's hand. What was
left of it clattered to the floor between his sneakers
and her penny loafers.

"He's thinking of leaving next week."

Luke watched Elaine's features crumple into
disappointment. He was a sick man to get pleasure
from her sorrow. But that sorrow was because she
thought he was leaving. It meant that she cared.

"The good news is," he continued, "with my job
as a writer, I can work from anywhere. Including
here."

The sadness didn't immediately melt away. It was
replaced with wariness. The same wariness from

when she'd awakened to find him in her hospital room.

"I'm working on my third book. I thought if you had the time, and since you finished the second book, you might look at the third book's draft to give me some feedback."

"I can do that," she said. She reached into the freezer for another ice cube. "You know, I thought you were going to introduce a love story by the way the second story ended."

"That's funny because I've been thinking about just that."

"The captain has been through a lot."

"I know she has."

"Her second in command has been so patient with her."

"Well," said Luke, ignoring the cold trickle of the melting ice between them, "he believes in her and would do anything to protect her."

"Yeah," said Elaine. "I got that as I was reading their story."

"Then you know he would never do anything to hurt her."

"I think I believe that," she said, her gaze locked on his. "But, still, I think you should probably take it slow. In the draft, I mean. You don't want the readers to get upset that there's now a love story where they hadn't expected one."

"You're right," said Luke. "We should take it slow."

Elaine parted her lips to respond. But before she could draw in the breath to get any words out, Luke's lips crashed into hers. The honey of her lips was sweeter than anything he'd ever tasted. Which was why it was pure agony to pull away from her as he winced in pain.

"Did I hurt you?" she said.

"Yeah," he grinned, brushing at the bruise from the football. "But, I'm fine."

He wasn't going to let a small injury like that keep him from what he wanted most in the world. Luke touched his lips to Elaine's again. Lightly this time.

He sipped at her, like a treat that had a hard exterior. Yet he knew that once he wore the outer shell down, the center was nothing but ooey-gooey goodness. And he was right.

Elaine was pure nectar at her center. It only took a few strokes of his bottom lip to wear her down. And then she melted into his arms.

Luke held her for long moments after their

kisses. She hid her face in his chest for a while. He allowed her to compose herself.

When she straightened, her smile was shy. "Walk me to my car?"

Luke did so, keeping her wrapped up in his arms. Wishing for the day when he would never have to let her go.

"About Sunday," she said.

Luke's heart stopped and then fumbled around in his chest. "Yeah?"

"I think I've had enough of ranch life today," she said. "Can it just be the two of us? Will you come to my place tomorrow?"

Luke chuckled, dipping his nose into her hair. This ranch was a lot to take in for a woman who preferred the quiet of the library stacks. "I'll be there."

"Dinner is at five o'clock sharp."

"I'll be there five minutes early."

Luke handed Elaine into her car. He waited until she was buckled in before he shut the door. With a small wave, she turned the engine on and pulled out.

He was on cloud nine as he walked back into the house. As he returned to the kitchen, aiming to clean up the two ice cubes that had turned to a small puddle of water on the floor, he noticed that the back door was open.

Luke closed the door and went in search of his guest. He assumed it had to be Paul. He found Paul in the bathroom. His broad body was bent over the toilet. His chest caved in as he heaved. Luke smelled the metallic tint before he saw the blood.

"I may have pushed it a little too hard," Paul said before his eyes rolled back in his head, and he passed out cold.

CHAPTER EIGHTEEN

"You can't make him a steak." Mary jerked back from the glass display as though there was a live cow mooing from the other side.

"Why not?" Elaine asked.

"Because any woman would make him a steak. That would show you are basic and not trying at all. The hard part of making a steak is picking the best cut from the butcher. So. if he wants to date the butcher, it's a go. No one can screw up a steak. We want to show some effort."

Elaine pushed her cart away from the red meat and came to the seafood section. "Scallops?"

"Oh, my gosh, no." Mary slapped her forehead.

"Do you want to have fish breath when he kisses you?"

No. Elaine definitely did not want fish breath. That would make him pull away from her, and she wanted Luke to pull her closer. She had been breathless after their first kiss. Heck, she'd been breathless during it.

She'd found herself collapsing into his chest and seeking refuge there. He'd held her to him. She'd never felt so safe, so secure. She wanted more of that.

What was happening between her and Luke, what was happening inside her, was scary. She'd seen scary when her parents fought. She'd seen warm when they were lovey-dovey.

Elaine didn't want scary. She wanted warm and lovey-dovey. So, she put the scallops back.

"And nothing with garlic." Mary smacked the back of Elaine's hand, forcing her to drop the bulb of garlic back into its display basket.

"I like garlic," Elaine said, cradling her hand. "I can't believe there are this many rules to a dinner date. Why don't I just text him what he wants."

Mary slapped the cell phone out of Elaine's hand. It clattered into the empty grocery cart. "Do not text him first. Do you want to seem eager?"

"I'm so confused?" Now Elaine cradled both of her hands to her chest, afraid of another rebuke from her friend. "I don't want to seem that I'm trying hard, but I actually want to try. I don't want to appear eager, even though I want him to kiss me again?"

"Yes," sighed Mary, as though she'd just experienced a breakthrough with a dunce of a student. "Now, you're getting it."

Wow, dating was hard. No wonder Elaine had never bothered.

"Duck," said Mary.

Elaine prepared to bend down and take cover. Then she saw the choice of meat in Mary's hands. "You want me to make him a duck dish?"

"With rosemary potatoes and buttered green beans. It shows a bit of effort, that you like fine things, and aren't cheap. But it also has a dash of homey and healthy baked in."

"This is so complicated," Elaine said, taking the duck and placing it into the basket.

"This is dating in the twenty-first century, honey."

"You're dating?" They looked up to find Juan. He wheeled a cart of mangos and avocados to a stop in front of them. "I've known you since we were kids.

This guy has known you less than a week. Now, you're going on a date with him?"

"Well ... He knows me differently," was all Elaine could manage to say. "He's the first guy to make me want more than a friendship."

She wanted the warm and safe, but she was willing to go through a bit of scary to get to it. She was willing to break her routine. But not who she was.

Elaine picked up the garlic bulb and tossed it into the cart in the face of Mary's ire. Luke had been patient with her. He'd accepted her with all her quirks. So, she was not going to hide the fact that she liked garlic. Besides, two garlic mouths canceled each other out. Right?

After leaving a dejected Juan, and a scowling Mary, Elaine went home and began cooking the garlic and rosemary duck dish. She also broke Mary's rule and texted Luke.

He didn't respond immediately. But she supposed he was driving. That was a good sign, he didn't text and drive.

The duck came out perfectly. She set the table with a set of mismatched dishes. Over the years, her mom had broken each set her dad brought home.

Elaine dimmed the lights. She had just enough

time to change and touch her makeup up. Pulling open the bathroom door, she noted the crack in the wood from a time when her mother slammed it in her father's face and refused to come out all day.

Elaine stared at herself in the bathroom mirror. She had her mother's eyes, her father's nose. But everything else was all her. She was her own person. She had let them keep her cooped up in this house all her life. She had never invited a man over because she was too afraid of the damage he might cause. That was changing tonight.

Walking out of the bathroom and into her bedroom, she saw *Tess of the d'Urbervilles* lying on her nightstand. Elaine had stopped reading the story after Angel had abandoned Tess when she told her deepest shame. Angel hadn't been able to deal, and he'd sailed away and out of her life, leaving his wife, the woman he'd promised to love and care for, practically destitute.

Elaine picked up *Tess*. She pulled out the bookmark, letting the pages shut without a marker. Turning to her closet, she put the book back on the shelf.

She knew how that story ended. She was looking forward to experiencing a different ending with her own love story. One where no secrets were kept. One where she and her Angel talked out any differences and tried to accept each other for who they were.

Elaine went downstairs to wait for Luke. Looking at the clock, she saw that he was five minutes late. She didn't panic. She thumbed her phone.

At fifteen minutes late, she put the duck back in the oven.

At thirty minutes late, she put the dishes in the fridge.

After an hour, she turned off the porch lights, scrubbed off her makeup, and climbed into bed.

uke woke with a start. Like he'd been pulled from a nightmare. It was dark, but he heard crashes and explosions in his head.

He looked around the room, trying to get his bearings. He wasn't in a war zone. It was light outside. Not an afternoon kind of light. More like the light of day. A new day.

He must have slept through the night. His body creaked and groaned from the awkward position he'd curled into in the night. He was in a hospital room. His large body folded into a small, uncomfortable chair.

Paul lay in the bed. There were wires and tubes going into his body. His heart monitor showed a steady beat. His chest rose and fell in a normal rhythm.

It was a normal scene. But it was one Luke had hoped he wouldn't have to witness ever again with his friend. The door opened, and the white-haired doctor walked in. His features were grim.

Luke swallowed. He inhaled through his nose, forcing the air to steel his insides before he heard the news. On the bed, Paul remained asleep. The man didn't have any remaining family. He'd long ago signed documents that Luke could hear details of his prognosis, but not make any decisions for him.

"Major Hanson is going to need surgery," said the doctor. "But he knows that."

Luke had suspected as much.

"It's going to take a lot of hard work, but I have every confidence that he'll make a full recovery if he elects to have the surgery. Otherwise, we might wind up back here in a few weeks or a few months."

"How long will the recovery take?" Luke asked. "If he does elect to do the surgery?"

"A year, at least."

When the doctor left the room, Luke let out the breath he'd used to steel himself. His body caved in on itself as he did so. He looked down at his friend.

Now that the doctor was no longer in the room, Paul's eyes were wide open.

Paul's gaze connected with Luke's and held. Luke wanted to look away. But his friend wouldn't let him. He knew where this conversation was about to go.

"Not your fault," said Paul.

"I know," Luke said. "That interception you caught was a foul, and you know it."

Paul let out a chuckle. That turned into a laugh. That turned into a guffaw. And then he winced.

Luke didn't go to him. He didn't reach out to his friend. He couldn't make any of this better for Paul. Paul had to make it better from himself.

That day in the war zone, Luke had done what he could to save his friend. He knew with perfect certainty had the roles been reversed that Paul would've done the same. In a heartbeat.

But Luke also knew that had the roles been reversed, he'd have gotten the necessary surgeries and done what was necessary to regain as much of his health as possible. Luke didn't understand Paul's hesitancy. He might never understand it. That didn't mean he was giving up on Paul.

"You're my family," said Luke. "You would've done the same for me. But you'd get on my nerves worse if I got injured."

"Debatable."

"I'm staying here, and so are you." Luke sat back down in the uncomfortable chair.

Paul twisted his lips before he spoke. "You're using me as an excuse to go to the town library."

Luke knew that was as close to an admission as he would ever get from his friend. Luke grinned. Then he frowned. Then he groaned. "Oh, no. I gotta go."

He'd not only missed their date. He'd missed an entire day as he waited for Paul to come out of the emergency room.

Luke floored it into town. He swung into an empty space at the library. Bursting into the front doors, he didn't see a cardigan-wearing bunhead behind the circulation desk.

"I rooted for you," said Mary, looking every bit the stern, banned-books type of librarian from his youth.

"There was an emergency," said Luke.

"It couldn't have been life or death."

"It was."

The stern look on Mary's face fell. "She's not here. She took the day off today. She never takes the day off."

That was all Luke needed to hear. He raced to

Elaine's home on foot, not wanting to deal with the traffic stops. Racing up the steps to her porch, he knocked.

He was about to knock a second time when the door opened, and there she was. Her hair was down. She wore a t-shirt with no cardigan. Elaine's face was impassive as she regarded him like she barely knew him.

"Let me explain," he said.

The smile that tugged at the corner of her mouth was not a pretty affair. "That's what my dad always said."

"Paul got hurt—"

"It doesn't matter."

"It does," Luke insisted. "I didn't mean to hurt you."

"But it did hurt," Elaine said. "Just like I thought it would. Imagine if I'd actually fallen in love with you."

That hit him straight in the heart. Because he was falling in love with her. He wanted to spend his days loving on her. He wanted to spend his time showing her what love could really be like. But more importantly, Luke wanted Elaine to not be afraid to fall in love with him.

"Don't back away from this," he said.

But she was shaking her head and backing away from the door. "It's not your fault. I'm just not built for this."

Luke could see the pain in her eyes. Once again, he'd hurt the one he cared about. He needed to regroup. He stepped to the side and heard a crash.

The pot he'd stepped into on their first night, the one that had spilled its innards, it was now broken into large pieces. The flower's leaves and bulbs crashed down onto the ground. The soil that had protected it was now slipping through the cracks of the porch and showing the plant's roots.

"I can fix it," he said.

"It doesn't matter. The cracks were already there."

Luke looked back to her. It was as though the life had gone out of her eyes, out of her very being. He wanted to reach out to her, to grab hold of her and pull her close, but she was too far away.

"Elaine, relationships aren't perfect. People make mistakes. I make mistakes. I use my body as cover to save the ones I care about. I don't always look before I cross the street."

She wouldn't meet his gaze. She looked suddenly weary and tired. Luke went to her, but she backed up behind the door. Her body stood rooted on the threshold, not letting him pass into her inner sanctuary.

"Let me try and fix this," he begged.

Elaine looked into his eyes. There was a tiny spark of hope. But mostly there was fear. And the fear won out.

"There are just too many cracks. It's not your fault." She shook her head, stepping back behind the door and closing it with a quiet snick.

But Luke wasn't giving up. Not on her. Not on them.

He picked up the pieces of the broken pot and backed down the steps.

CHAPTER TWENTY

She'd made a good decision with the duck. And the garlic, with its pungent and aromatic spiciness, was the perfect added touch to the leftovers of the dish. Elaine let out a sigh. The fiery kick from the bulbous onion on her breath knocked her back down on her pillow.

She checked her phone, but like the last two days, it was silent. He hadn't texted, or called, or come by again. Elaine realized she was a hypocrite because she desperately wanted him to. The silence that resulted from Luke's lack of presence in her life was driving her crazy.

Elaine used to crave the quiet when her parents fought. To tune them out while they went at it, she'd lose herself in a book. Most of the time, she got lost in a story where she already knew the ending, finding safety and security in the familiarity of the pages.

Right now, Elaine wanted to hear Luke's voice. Even if he yelled, which he'd never done. She wanted to sit at dinner with him. Even if he hated her cooking, which her full belly and garlic coated tongue reminded her was excellent. She wanted him to come through the door. Even if he slammed it behind him, which he hadn't done. He'd stepped back as she quietly closed the door in his face.

Because Luke wouldn't do any of those things. From the very first moment, since she'd opened her eyes and found him sitting beside her in the hospital room, he'd listened to her. Even when he disagreed with her decisions, he still respected her wishes. He'd thought of her safety first, but her comfort had been paramount.

Except for the one time when he'd let her down for dinner.

But he'd come to her. He'd apologized to her. He'd wanted to make it right with her. She was the one who had turned him away.

It had to have been something big that had kept him away from their date. He'd looked tired when he'd come to her. Worn out. Weary. Like he hadn't slept the night before.

He'd said that Paul had gotten hurt. Where had they been? What had happened to put those bags under his eyes? What could she do to take his stress away?

Elaine didn't have the answers. And if her silent phone had anything to say about it, she wasn't going to get the answers anytime soon. She'd shoved Luke out of her life, and like the considerate person he was, he was going to respect her wishes.

Elaine wanted to make another wish. But what would she wish for? That he'd come to her again last night? That he was perfect and wouldn't make any mistakes in the future? That he had never hurt her?

It was an impossible feat. Relationships were messy. But Luke hadn't made anywhere near a mess like her parents had.

Needing some sort of action in her indecision, Elaine got out of bed. The sun shone into her bedroom window, announcing a new day. She reached for the curtains, intent on closing out the happy star when she saw something on her porch.

Leaving the curtains wide open, Elaine raced down the stairs. She flung the door open and had to immediately throw her arms up over her face. The sun's rays tackled her with their warmth, and her eyes weren't ready for it.

It didn't matter. When she managed to pull her hands away from shielding her eyes, she saw that he wasn't there. What was there was her potted plant. The one he'd accidentally broken. It looked whole again.

Picking up the pot, she saw that it wasn't entirely intact. There were still cracks in the ceramic. But he'd done his best to piece the broken parts back together. Inside the pot, the flower stood strong. It's leaves outstretched as though it were offering her a hug. The bud was opened, showing its petals, offering its most vulnerable part to her, as though it had never realized it had been through a battle.

Elaine's father would've replaced the pot. Her mother would've pretended it had never happened. Not Luke. He'd fixed it. Because that's the kind of man he was. He fixed what was broken.

Elaine looked down to see that the fixed pot wasn't the only thing Luke had left for her. A thick envelope lay on the welcome mat at her doorstep. By the heft and size of it, she knew there was a ream of paper inside.

Opening the package, she found the manuscript for Walker Skye's third book.

Elaine put the pot down. She dusted the nonexistent specs of dirt from her hands. Then she lifted the title page and carefully turned to the next page.

She'd expected to see Chapter One. That wasn't what was on the page. The Dedication made her heart stop, restart, and then fall.

For Elaine, it read, *who is worth fighting for.*

She stared at the words for a long time. Then she looked up. When she did, she could feel the hope in her eyes. But gazing up and down the streets, she saw that they were still empty.

Elaine had read hundreds of books. She'd gotten lost in countless stories. She'd imagined herself as dozens of heroines, even a few villains. This was the first time she was actually on a printed page.

Turning to the next page, she was immediately sucked into the story. By the end of the first page, she was well and truly hooked. By the end of the first act, she could no longer deny it.

Just like the heroine in the book, Elaine was truly, deeply in love with the commander of her heart. The second in command in the book had just put himself in the line of fire for the captain. The question was, were both the captain and Elaine brave enough to go into the battlefield to get the love they both wanted.

Elaine didn't turn to the page to find out. She set the book down, without a bookmark, and headed out of the door.

CHAPTER TWENTY-ONE

Luke looked down at his phone. There were new messages there, but they were from his agent asking about the manuscript. For the third time this week, Luke put the agent off. He wasn't prepared to show anyone the book, not until he learned what Elaine thought of the ending.

He'd left the book on her porch the other day. He hadn't heard anything back from her. But he'd already decided he wasn't giving up. Not on her. Not on what they could be.

"It's good," said Paul.

The man lay in the hospital bed. He was immobile after his surgery. Surprisingly, he was in good spirits. But that's what relieving chronic pain tended to do.

Luke kept his mouth shut on that opinion. The doctors expected Paul to make a full recovery. In time.

Luke had sent the first draft of the book to Elaine. But he'd also left a copy for Paul. His best friend had always been his first reader. Paul's vote of confidence was up there with Elaine's. Although his and Paul's future relationship wasn't hanging in the balance.

"Really?" said Luke. "You liked it?"

Paul nodded.

"Even though the hero doesn't get the girl?"

"It true to the character's growth," said Paul. "The two of them are just at the beginning of things. They both have a lot of scars that need to heal."

The second in command had offered himself up as a sacrifice for the captain. But she'd come to his rescue, blasting the enemy with her phaser. Her most trusted soldier had raced to her, swaggered was how Luke had described it on the page.

After he'd kissed her, she'd pushed him away. Both the captain and her creator knew she wasn't ready to receive love. Not yet. But it had awakened something in her, something she wanted to fight for.

Just like the captain did with every battle, she

would be methodical about it. She would be thoughtful. She would work on her plan.

The plan was to help her new love interest heal the wounds he'd sustained in battle, the wounds she'd tried to protect him from. She'd learned that she couldn't protect the people she loved from hardships. All she could do was stand by them, help them heal.

"You realize I'm in the recovery wing of the hospital," said Paul. "I'm in the healing process. Your librarian is still out there on the battlefield."

Luke scrubbed a hand over his face. He wanted nothing more than to charge back into the minefield that was Elaine's past and slay all her demons. It had killed him to leave her at the door the other day. She'd looked so lost and in need. But he knew she wouldn't reach out to him. She was still too wounded to even lift her hand.

"I'm going to have to be patient with her," Luke said. Just like the heroine he penned, the female main character in his real-life wasn't ready to receive love. But he was certain something had awakened inside her. He needed to be methodical about his next move. "I have a plan. I need to show her I'm not going anywhere."

Paul made a sound of disbelief. "You crowded me when I got injured. You bullied me into this treatment. You've been nothing short of a helicopter parent. But she gets space to make her own decisions?"

"Yeah." Luke shrugged. "You can't outrun me. I don't want to scare her off."

Paul tossed a pillow at Luke's head. Luke easily dodged. When he straightened, both men chuckled.

When Paul sobered, he stared his best friend straight into the eye and asked the million-dollar question. "What are you doing here babysitting me? Go annoy her into submission."

That wasn't part of the plan. He needed to give her time. He knew Elaine was it for him. He knew it in his bones. Just as he'd known that he and Paul would be more than military brothers.

"It's been two days," said Paul. "She could use a little nudge. Plus, I need to get my beauty sleep."

Maybe Paul was right. Maybe Luke could just stop by her house and check on her? Or stroll by the library. It was Taco Tuesday and getting close to noon. He knew where she'd be.

"And then get to work on the final book so that captain and her boy toy can finally get together."

Yeah. Luke was eager to write that book. But before that, he needed to pen his own final chapter. He was ready for his own happily ever after. He was ready for the battle to be over.

He headed out of the hospital and down the main street. He pulled out his phone and pulled up Elaine's number. Before hitting her contact, he made sure to look both ways at the intersection. And there she was.

Elaine stood on the other side of the street, looking down at her phone. Her fingers worked furiously. Luke watched as she took a deep breath and then hit one final key.

A second later, he startled as his phone chimed. Her fingers had moved so fast, so furious, for a long stretch. But her message was simple.

I made a mistake. Will you give me another chance?

Instead of replying, Luke looked up from his phone. He'd hoped to catch her gaze, but she was looking down at her phone. Her gaze was intent as she waited. She cradled the device in both her hands, as though afraid she'd drop it.

Luke took a step into the street, only to jerk his foot back when the screech of a honking horn demanded his attention.

Elaine looked up then. She caught his gaze. Her features broke into a beautiful smile, brighter than the sun.

She stepped a foot into the street, only to jerk back when another vehicle honked at her.

Looking up to the street lights, Luke saw the white walking man flashing on the opposite street. The orange numbers counted down, telling him that he only needed to wait another twenty seconds before he could get to her.

It was too long.

Luke held out his hand, strong-arming the cars on the road to stop for him. He was able to make it safely across to her in under five seconds.

He had a carefully calculated plan. It all went out the window the moment he was standing at her feet. Without waiting for a protest, he brought his lips to hers.

Just like she had the first time he'd kissed her, Elaine melted into his arms. She opened to him. She opened for him. Without any words between them, Luke knew that the healing process had begun. Not just for her, but for him as well.

"I'm sorry," she said when he let her up for air. "I don't know how to do this. I said I'd never do this. And now that I'm here, I'm just so scared."

"I've got you," he said, pulling her closer to him. "I'm not going to leave you. I'm never going to leave you. Even if you want to read Hardy to me every night, I'll still be here in the morning."

That got a small smile out of her. Then she gulped. "So, we're going to do this? We're going to date?"

"Date?" Luke grinned, biting his tongue and the proposal that was right at the tip of it. "Yes, we're going to date. How about I buy you a taco?"

"I'd like that."

Luke offered Elaine his arm. Just like something out of the Victorian era books that she liked. When she took it, he swaggered into the restaurant, just like the heroes of the military science fiction books and movies that he liked.

From behind the counter, Juan glared at the two of them. Luke let it slide. He had time to win the chef over. As long as the man realized the battle for Elaine had been fought and won. Because like he said, he wasn't going anywhere.

More books are coming from the Purple Heart Ranch. Be sure and sign up for Shanae's mailing list to find out when, to receive early excerpts, and to read free short stories from the ranch that aren't available anywhere else!

http://bit.ly/ShanaeJohnsonReaders

Shanae Johnson was raised by Saturday Morning cartoons and After School Specials. She still doesn't understand why there isn't a life lesson that ties the issues of the day together just before bedtime. While she's still waiting for the meaning of it all, she writes stories to try and figure it all out. Her books are wholesome and sweet, but her are heroes are hot and heroines are full of sass!

And by the way, the E elongates the A. So it's pronounced Shan-aaaaaaaa. Perfect for a hero to call out across the moors, or up to a balcony, or to blare outside her window on a boombox. If you hear him calling her name, please send him her way!

You can sign up for Shanae's Reader Group at http://bit.ly/ShanaeJohnsonReaders

Also By Shanae Johnson

The Brides of Purple Heart

On His Bended Knee

Hand Over His Heart

Offering His Arm

His Permanent Scar

Having His Back

In Over His Head

Always On His Mind

Every Step He Takes

In His Good Hands

Light Up His Life

Strength to Stand

The Rangers of Purple Heart

The Rancher takes his Convenient Bride

The Rancher takes his Best Friend's Sister

The Rancher takes his Runaway Bride

The Rancher takes his Star Crossed Love

The Rancher takes his Love at First Sight

The Rancher takes his Last Chance at Love

The Rebel Royals series

The King and the Kindergarten Teacher

The Prince and the Pie Maker

The Duke and the DJ